A R

Curiou

By Patrick Forsyth

This Edition Published by Stanhope Books, Hertfordshire, UK 2020

www.stanhopebooks.com

Cover design and format by Patrick Forsyth & Lloyd Bonson © 2020

ISBN-13: 978-1-909893-29-0

Dedication

Again in memory of Sue: my writing is no longer constantly interrupted, I so miss that…

…… but would not have had it any other way.

`

PROLOGUE

It was time

He was angry. So angry. He told himself it was a natural reaction, but it certainly affected his state of mind. He knew he was not operating in his usual calm, rational manner. It was unnerving. He found himself losing his temper over small things that would normally be dismissed and surmounted in a moment. As time went by the feeling gradually subsided, but the underlying cause remained. That would never go away. Nevertheless bit by bit his feelings changed, his anger diminished to be replaced by a calmer state of mind and he reckoned he had now begun to think straight about things; certainly he not only coped with his routine activities again but had time for what he believed was rational thought about the future.

The resolve came first. A personal commitment to do something about it. The question was what to do. As time continued to pass he observed that various things had been tried and so far, there had been no reaction and no change had been evident. He decided that he was not prepared to let it go, he had promised himself that, and now it seemed he must do something, something radical, something that worked, and that would act to change things.

He considered a range of different ideas, rejecting most at an early stage as impractical or impossible. Then gradually a single idea took hold, one that needed thinking through, but which he felt had possibilities. Real possibilities. As he ran over the implications in his mind he added in details, and still it seemed to be possible. There were risks, of course there were, and some elements of the plan were not ideal, but that too seemed to be inevitable. Besides he could think of nothing that was totally without downsides. So he began to work out the details, he made notes, and finally a real plan seemed to be coming together.

At last he felt he had an idea that would get all the results he wanted, he accepted that it was not without risks, he had catalogued those along the way, but he was convinced it was a sound plan. His certainty of being able to make it work grew. Desperate measures perhaps, but he concluded that such was the only way to go. He convinced himself he could make it work, he resolved to carry it out.

He was absolute in his determination: it was time to make them pay.

CHAPTER ONE

Maybe this was the one

Bob Norton had worked at the paper for more than ten years. Local papers had suffered in recent times, like so many other changed businesses their woes lay primarily at the door of the way the internet had developed. Much advertising that used to both fill out their pages and add to their revenue had gone online. Nevertheless Bob honestly believed the local paper was an institution at the heart of a community, certainly the *Maldon Express* had been forced to trim its sails a little in recent times but it continued, and in Bob's view it continued very well. He was an enthusiast: his office bore testament to this, the space around him was totally filled with things to do with words. There were multiple shelves of books, including a significant number of reference books ranging from dictionaries to books about the local area. Every available wall surface, much of which was in the form of pin boards, was covered with paper, everything from the ubiquitous yellow sticky note to whole pages from the Express and other newspapers. His desk matched the office, as well as a computer and monitor, so many piles of paper ranged across its surface that it was virtually impossible to see what the desk top was made of as none of it was visible. Nevertheless, as his staff could testify, he seemed able to locate anything in a moment as he plunged with precision into an unlabelled pile to produce exactly what was required. He certainly worked at his editorship and managed the whole role in a way that succeeded in creating a well-regarded paper.

His small team worked well together, both on the editorial side and on obtaining advertising from those advertisers who still favoured their particular form of media. In terms of personnel the advertising side was more stable, the reporters on the other hand did not tend to stay so long, such people always seemed keen to work on a bigger paper – preferably a national – or they moved on to the safer environment of magazines. One such change was coming up. Debbie had only been with the Express just over a year but very much wanted to work, and live, in London; recently she had succeeded in getting a job on a women's magazine, given in her notice and would be leaving shortly. Bob was annoyed, he rated her as good, he would have been happy for her to stay, but realistically he recognised how things were and that even more money, which in any case the paper could not afford, would not tempt her to remain. He resolved therefore that it was recruitment time. This was not his favourite job, it was always a time consuming and uncertain process. He would love to find someone who would stay longer, a potential assistant editor even, and someone who would be as passionate about a local paper as he was.

Despite his feelings about internet advertising it was to the internet that he turned, albeit after an ad in their own pages had not produced any suitable candidates - he had interviewed no one. Too many people, Bob thought, just liked the idea of journalism, but did not seem to have any real passion for writing. The internet notification, however, produced a number of candidates, four of which he felt were worth a look. He asked those four to fill in an application form. Perhaps Bob was old fashioned in this respect, but he liked to see that a candidate was prepared to spend a little time completing this; he found the information they gathered was helpful and it also provided a good way to compare one candidate with another on a similar basis.

As he dwelt on the matter, Becky, who acted as his secretary and also as receptionist, appeared at his door, which he always tended to leave ajar as he liked to know what was going on in the open office next to him where most of his team were seated.

"I've opened up the morning post Bob," she said and placed a number of sheets on his desk. "There are two of the application forms back from potential replacements for Debbie."

"Thanks, Becky, I dare say the rest is bills; I'll have a look." Most things of any importance came by email these days. The recruitment situation was becoming more urgent, two of the four interesting applications, the ones received first, had so far failed to return a form, something that Bob regarded as a bad sign. Anyone not doing this promptly, Bob believed, sent out a clear, unspoken negative message, indeed some such would probably not do it at all preferring to pursue other options they perhaps saw as easier. He thumbed through the papers Becky had handed over to him and had a look.

David Bartholomew's application had initially seemed a good one. Now he looked at his form he wondered. His handwriting was even worse than the style traditionally attributed to many a doctor. Worse, his heart did not seem to be in it; several sections of the form were blank, several questions designed to actually get a candidate to say something about themselves were answered with a single short sentence or merely a phrase. There was no clue as to why the applicant suddenly wanted to work for a newspaper. He currently worked for an insurance company with which there seemed to be no obvious link, and Bob was generally not enthused by what he saw. He wondered why he had sent the man a form.

The second application form looked much more like what he wanted; maybe this was the one, he thought. Alice Carter had left university with a decent degree just recently, she was working part time in a bookshop while she hunted for what she described as "a job where I can put my love of writing usefully to work". Her form was fully completed, the sections that he wanted to be completed with some reasonable detail did just that, and a passion for writing seemed to shine through. She had attached a couple of examples of her writing from a university magazine and he liked what he saw. He increasingly thought she could be the one. He took her form out to Becky at her desk.

"I am not sure about the other one, leave that with me, but can you fix for this one to come to an interview. As soon as possible, Debbie's due to leave before too long."

"Okay, I'll do it as soon as I can make contact with her." Becky looked at the name on the form as she spoke and got the gender right. Bob thanked her and went back to his office. He reread one of the articles that had accompanied Alice's application and which still remained on his desk. Yes, he thought this one was worth pursuing, although he did not pin his hopes on it, these days sometimes a candidate with an interview scheduled not only failed to turn up but also failed to get in touch to say they were not coming or give any reason for dropping out. He shouted out to the outer office.

"Debbie, spare me a moment would you." Debbie duly came into his office a few moments later.

"Right, Debbie, I'm conscious that we do not have you with us for much longer and it looks like you may be gone before a successor is appointed, so you and I should perhaps go through some sort of handover. I need to know everything longer term that's on your desk as it were and that will need handing over to someone else. And currently it seems it may well have to come to me." Debbie said she understood and they arranged for her to get things together and for them to meet again in the afternoon. Bob went back to work, amongst the many organisational and management tasks he had he did need to do some actual writing. He opened a new document on his computer and began to consider the current week's editorial, which, given the importance of visitors to the town, he quickly decided had to link to the coming summer season. He had just got going when his phone rang, it was Becky.

"All fixed, she was not at work today, and I've arranged for Alice Carter to be here at 11.00 am on Tuesday. Okay?" Bob acknowledged that it was. He did not want to appoint anyone below par, but the need for a new reporter was becoming urgent. However, he had a good feeling about Alice and, whoever he appointed, he rather looked forward to running in someone new. It could be a tough process to get someone into shape, but if someone was willing to learn they would he believed find it a rewarding job.

He made a note of the time of the appointment in his diary, before returning to his writing.

CHAPTER TWO
Only a small matter

Six months ago I was not a reporter and I did not even know where the town of Maldon was located. For the record it's an attractive small town about five miles off the A 12, which runs north out of London, and is situated between Chelmsford and Colchester and it's where I now call home. It was the job I wanted, not the location, but the location is fine.

I suppose I was always what you might call bookish and I always wanted to write; from quite a young age I spent much time writing stories, diaries and rants against things I hated. My favourite present was a good fat exercise book and I rejoiced the day I could start to use a computer. Later, at university, I spent more time editing a university magazine than I did on my degree, though I got a 2.1 in English in the end. Then I had to get a job and that proved difficult. There are so many graduates these days, job hunting is a highly competitive process in many fields and journalism is no exception. I went on line, I wrote letters, I even knocked on doors, but for a while I did so with no result. Well, I got two interviews from about thirty possibilities: one didn't like me and one I didn't like. I continued to live at home and did shifts working part time in a book shop to help finance my ongoing job search. My parents demanded no rent and my mother continued to do my washing. I told myself it would not be long until I had a job, was earning and had my independence.

I cast the net quite wide and finally, an application in response to an advertisement I saw online for a post at the *Maldon Express* got me an interview. I travelled into and through central London from the family home on the southern fringes of the capital and went to meet Bob Norton in an office above a shop in Maldon High Street. I got parked in what I now know is the town's main car park and Mr Google told me the newspaper's office was only two or three minutes' walk away. They wanted what used to be called a "cub" reporter, a trainee, or rather, let's be frank – a dogsbody. Once there I spoke first to the receptionist and was shown promptly into the editor's office. I hoped it might impress him that I had read the paper, his paper that is, I brought a copy with me to the interview and sat down holding it in my lap together with a notebook. The paper took a bit of getting hold of, Maldon is the best part of a hundred miles away from where I live and I had to telephone three shops before I found one that would post me a copy. I wore my "interview outfit", somewhat smarter than my customary jeans. Before I went in I had found a loo in a nearby Costa Coffee shop in which to try to tame my naturally unruly hair, it's what one hairdresser once described as the wrong sort of blond, and I resolved not to push my glasses up my nose so often that it gets commented on. I am not sure whether it is the frames or my nose that prompt it, but it has certainly become a habit.

Bob Norton, he told me at once to call him Bob, was probably in his late-forties and very business-like. His cluttered office was at the back of the building away from the street, the windows showed an unattractive view of buildings and part of a car park. On the other side of the room the top half of the wall facing onto the open office beyond was made of glass allowing him to see his team at work. There was paper everywhere, he even had to move a pile of files before I could sit down. After the usual sorts of initial questions on topics apparently picked at random off my CV, he suggested I actually write something. There and then. Well, I hadn't expected that; a test. I'd skipped describing my childhood stories but I'd shown him some stuff I wrote for the university magazine and a couple of articles I'd had published in a woman's magazine; over the last few months I had begun to do a little freelance writing. Anyway he sat me down at a computer, gave me a story, something about a pub being taken over by the community in a small village and left me to it. The instruction was to write my own version of it in half the original number of words.

"Half an hour sufficient? I don't want to rush you, though of course we often have to work against the clock." I agreed.

He's thorough, I'll give him that. I made a few quick notes (I was glad I had brought my notebook), struggled a little with the unfamiliar keyboard and managed to write something, read it over and print it out before he called me back to his office.

He sat and read over what I had written apparently doing so with very great concentration. Then the phone on his desk rang, interrupting the process, he signalled for me to stay put and had a brief conversation that was something to do with print. Any feeling I had for the interview evaporated by then as it had moved away from the question and answer format of the typical interview; I was just not sure how it had been going. I waited patiently while he spoke on the phone and pretended to look at my copy of the newspaper, which I had already read from cover to cover. Then he ended the phone call and was back with me.

"Well, that's not bad. I'm prepared to give it a go if you are. For a trial period of course. Yes or no?" I found that I was apparently being offered a job. On the spot. I said yes, well what I actually said was "Yes, thank you very much." He rattled through a few details: salary, pitiful but about what I expected; holidays, not for a while, in fact not until my trial period was up; starting date, Monday, that was less than one week on; and we were done. I'd got the job, not much money and a trial before it's confirmed, but it was a start. I looked forward to becoming a reporter.

First I had to find somewhere local to live. I left the office and considered the typical small town High Street onto which I emerged. I was to discover later that it is not so typical, the mixture of independent and chain shops offers a fair old mixture of offerings and more places to have a cuppa and cake than you can shake a stick at. I picked a direction at random and walked up a slight hill with a church visible ahead of me. I went into the first estate agency I came to and asked about renting somewhere to live. I doubted I could find anything in any way permanent at the stage I was at, so I opted for specifying only whatever was least expensive and most central. They only had one place that seemed in any way suitable, a tiny "studio apartment" (much too grand a description as it transpired), which I viewed and signed up for there and then. It was in a fair sized two story house where the owner, a widow who I discovered had converted the house after her husband died, lived on the ground floor above which was a flat and what would be my tiny abode. Small it might have been, but it was clean, comfortable and well furnished.

She gave me a cup of tea, she took a shine to my story I think, and we arranged as she put it "something of an informal arrangement until that new job of yours is made permanent". When I left she promised me that she would buy the local paper in future. It was a lucky break amongst others in a day that had turned out well. I phoned home with the news before making the long drive back. Even the traffic on my route home was reasonably kind to me.

CHAPTER THREE

It was ready

Desperate measures: that had become a mantra for him as he planned. He had concluded that it was the only way to go. Various things had been tried and so far, there had still been no reaction and no change had been evident. He was not prepared to let it go, he had promised himself that, and now it seemed he must do something radical, something that worked, that would change things. And at last he felt he had an idea that would get results, he accepted that it was not without risk but he was convinced it was a sound plan.

He was tired. Setting everything up had taken it out of him if he was honest, but the plan was made as were most of the preparations and it was now all but ready to go in just a few days' time.

He had to get the last arrangements finished quickly now as he had thought of an ideal time to put his plan into action. He had only a little more to do. The arrangements had included a fair amount of shopping and also some DIY. The shopping had taken him to outlets with which he was not familiar and the DIY, which had never been his forte, had certainly taxed his meagre talents in that respect. He had bought some new tools to help, but the necessary tasks had spread across a couple of weeks before everything was sorted. Needing to buy some stuff that he had never had need of before, he had started by working out where to purchase things. Other stuff was straightforward but he had sourced items from a variety of stores and done so across a wide area rather than just at outlets near his home. He had not wanted to draw attention to himself.

Now he sat for a moment in the centre of the room and looked around, making a final check. All seemed to be as he wanted, as he had planned. The room was, or had been, very ordinary, and appeared not to have been used for some years previously. Once a spare bedroom or perhaps a storeroom, a dumping ground as his wife had always referred to such spaces, now it looked a little different. In some ways it remained ordinary looking, a typical upstairs bedroom of the sort an estate agent could genuinely describe as a double; but it was the details that mattered. He had started out by filling three pages of a notebook with a list of what was required and of the timing; the timing was going to be important, crucial in fact if all was to go to plan. He grouped his purchases by category and got everything together. Now all the different pieces were in place just so. He was satisfied that he had thought of everything. He could move on, he just had some messages to write and then needed to make precise arrangements for their delivery.

The bedroom window had given him the greatest problem. The screens had had to be made to measure but they had then had to be installed with care, not least as, being made of metal, they were heavy. He had done this himself, he had wanted no one else involved. It had been a bit of a struggle, indeed the supplier had said it would be and was surprised that he wouldn't retain their installers to put them up. Now installed they made the room somewhat dark, so he had put stronger bulbs in the lights and added an extra lamp on the bedside table. But in time he had done everything and it was all now secure.

He took a moment getting up from the chair, went to the door and left the room, he stood on the landing and turned the key in the bedroom door, then swung round and headed down the stairs, going to the kitchen and making a cup of tea before moving on. Tea drunk, he put on his coat ready to go out and picked up the two reusable shopping bags he had brought to take with him to the supermarket. Domestic chores did not stop just because one was busy with a project. As he walked across the hall to the front door he paused for a moment and glanced back up the stairs.

It was ready, he thought to himself, and he felt confident that no one would be able to escape from that room.

CHAPTER FOUR

Quite a satisfying result

It's the best part of six months since I was hired and as Christmas approaches, I am spending a moment taking stock. It's true to say that for some of my time I really am a reporter, though I also make a great many cups of tea. And coffee, black with two sugars for Bob. I run errands, and I am getting to know the town and its surrounds as I get out and about. I like it here too: Maldon's on the River Blackwater – the estuary – and known for being the prime home of the famous old fashioned Thames sailing barges, some of which still operate commercially in a touristy kind of way giving trips to bird watchers and the like, despite them being over a hundred years old.

In his role as editor Bob runs a tight ship and does so working with a small team, both busy preparing the weekly paper and dealing with the advertising it carries – advertising revenue being vital to the commercial success of any local paper - all of whom he keeps busy. Local newspapers have to watch the pennies in recent times, something Bob drums into us on nearly a daily basis, so we are certainly not overstaffed. I am getting used to Bob's way of operating, which in my case is very dictatorial, but I am writing more and more of late. Early on everything I wrote came back daubed with fierce looking red marks, but I'm a fast learner and soon got the hang of how Bob wanted things done. I am learning a lot.

As time has gone by I have wanted more and more to deal with something bigger than the stories currently allocated to me. Meantime no one, but no one, can describe a church fete or sale of work better than I can, but I increasingly want more.

*

Today I am sitting at my desk checking over the draft of what I hope will prove to be some truly deathless prose, when I hear a now familiar shout. It's 4.30 and I was beginning to think about going home.

"Alice, here to me." I get up from my cubicle, it's actually just a desk with a head high barrier in front of it to screen it from another similar desk arranged facing it, and go to Bob's office. Much that he passes over needs little discussion so I stand at the door rather than going to sit down.

"There's a Mrs McKeith coming into the office in a couple of minutes, I have given her your name, something about a dog, see what's what will you. If there is anything to write up do it quick, we are up against the weekly deadline." No need to sit down, I mutter that of course I will and go back to my desk to find my phone rings almost as I sit down.

"Mrs McKeith's here at the front desk for you." It's Becky.

My desk faces away from the entrance so I did not see the lady arrive. I go and greet her and sit her down alongside my desk; the paper being run on a shoestring we do not have the luxury of separate meeting rooms, only the editor has the privacy of his own office and that's hardly palatial. The demographics in Maldon veer towards the older end of the population scale and include a large number of retired people of which this lady is clearly one. She's left her coat hanging by the office entrance and is wearing a smart blue two piece suit in what my mother calls a herringbone pattern and has a pair of large spectacles hanging round her neck on a gold coloured chain. Her hair is still dark but its style looks a bit like an experiment that did not completely work out. I sit her down and introduce myself and set out to discover what she wants.

"So, what's this all about, how can I help Mrs McKeith?" Before answering she insists I call her Mary.

"I do hope you can help. It's my dog, Betty. Someone's stolen her. It's terrible, I'm on my own, she's such a good companion and I'll miss her so much." The story this describes doesn't fill my heart with joy, but she's a nice enough lady so I go with it and ask some questions.

"When was this? How did it happen? Have you told the police?" Straight to the point.

"It was late this morning in the front garden. I had just got back from the corner shops and was carrying a bag with some shopping in it. I let go of the dog, put the bag down and got the door open. It probably took a moment, the key sometimes sticks you see, I took the bag inside, went back for Betty and she was gone. She still had her lead on. Stolen right out of my garden just behind me, I mean what's the world coming to?"

"And the police?"

"Yes, I told them right away, well after I had looked up and down the road of course, they were nice enough but I know they don't see something like this as a priority. But it is for me, a priority that is, can you put a picture in the paper? Someone may see her with someone else." She says the words "someone else" through gritted teeth. Bob had reminded me that today's deadline day, but having been here a while now I know the form, I can probably get something in if I'm quick and photos are always good, though there will not be the time or space for very many words. I tell Mrs McKeith, Mary, what I can do, though I don't promise anything specific, and accept the photograph of Betty which she proffers. It's not my sort of dog. Rather too small, we had a black cocker spaniel when I was a child and I have always thought that anything smaller than that was not a proper dog. However, this black and white mongrel terrier sort of thingy was no doubt important to its owner though, so I promise to do what I can and send Mary on her way.

"I know it's only a small matter, my dear, but it's truly important to me, thank you so much. Oh, and I will be sure to buy a copy of the next edition." Important: the dictionary says that means "of great effect or consequence, momentous" – I rather think momentous describes it well for Mrs McKeith, that little dog is a central part of her life. She gives me her address and telephone number so that anyone who might find the dog can call her. I scan the picture into my computer, write a few words and see it off into production just in time for it to appear in the coming edition. I do not put in her contact details, these days that could lead to all sorts of difficulties, but I write that anyone with any information about the dog should make contact with the newspaper office. If that should happen we can then put them in touch.

*

Two days later a man telephones the office to say that he has found that dog wandering, still attached to her lead, a couple of miles along a footpath from where Mary lives. When found the lead was tangled up in some brambles and the dog could not go home even assuming she could find her way. Becky gives me the message and I put the finder and Mary in touch, I assume the dog will soon be reunited with its owner, and think no more about it. It is not, after all, the greatest story I have ever written, nor indeed did the piece even have my name on it. Tiny items don't usually warrant a byline, so a proportion of what I write gets no credit. Nevertheless I think it's quite a satisfying result and I reckon Mary McKeith is delighted as Becky told me later that she had telephoned to say that she thinks both I and the paper are "just the best".

*

I was right, Mary does think I'm wonderful, today I received a bunch of flowers at the office together with a handwritten note from my dog lady thanking me for acting to get her beloved Betty back safe, sound and doubtless ready to yap again. She really does think that we, and me in particular, acted to save the day. My goodness, the power of the press! I reckon the dog just wandered off on its own, but I wouldn't tell her that. I put the flowers in a jar and place them on the reception counter, after all it was the paper that got the result. Seems fair, and it brightens up the place a bit. Christmas is not far away, but our office decorations are minimal, I think the artificial Christmas tree that stands at the front of the office has probably served its purpose for more years than I have been alive. I suppose it's a gesture but it has certainly seen better days.

The dog incident makes me think though. If I'm honest that was probably the highlight of my week: a story consisting of less than a hundred words, no byline and an image of a lost dog in a photograph I did not take myself. It is surely about time I got my teeth into something a bit more – well, meaty, but my beloved editor is not seeing my talents in that sort of way as yet. I will have to see what tomorrow brings, but if there is not a change soon then maybe I should be looking to move on. Meantime I guess I must be persistent and work at it... and I really must look for new accommodation; I have to have a bit more space.

CHAPTER FIVE

All in good hands

Margaret liked her job at the library, she loved reading and books and although some of the activities she was involved in were routine, opening up, checking books in and out, answering queries and so on, her boss Philip Marchington was passionate about libraries and that was apparent in the way he ran things. He thus did his best to enthuse his small team and make sure that everyone had interesting things to do; Margaret reckoned he was a good sort of boss for whom to work. A current project was a story writing competition for children which had been planned, like many things that the library did, to focus attention on both learning to and enjoying reading. And Philip had asked her to make all the arrangements for it, from its announcement to the prize giving.

"It's a project that involves a good few elements, but I am sure you can cope, perhaps take things chronologically and create a checklist to start, right?"

First, she needed a judge, ideally a writer who was a bit of a name, but who would accept the need to spend a certain amount of time on reading entries and picking out the best ones in return only for a bit of publicity for their own writing. Margaret did not know of a children's writer who lived locally, but she was surrounded by booklovers on a daily basis. One of the library's regular activities was providing multiple copies of books for a variety of reading groups, their leaders came in regularly to collect copies of their next title and Margaret asked several of them if they could think of anyone suitable. Finally one such member was very specific.

"I am sure Eve Watson would be ideal, I am sure she's well qualified for it and would be prepared to spend the necessary time on it too. I don't know her address, but I do know she lives nearby, somewhere over towards Burnham, I think. My grandchildren love her books and I know you have some here in the library." That last comment seemed to be the ultimate recommendation. Margaret had the library all round her, she found one of Eve Watson's books – titled *Upside down magic* it was a book that naturally had its title appearing twice on the cover: once right way up and once upside down. She telephoned its publisher, who wanted to know why she wanted to get in touch with their author, then after she explained briefly, presumably regarding her reason as a worthy cause, they agreed to help put her in touch. While they would not give out her telephone number or email address, blaming this on data protection legislation, they did promise however to get in touch and put the idea to her so that she could contact the library should she wish. A couple of days later she phoned and Margaret explained the details of the competition and what was required of the judge. Eve was immediately keen.

"Yes, I think I could do that, I am flattered that you should ask me. Can you tell me about the timing: when would I get the entries and how long would I have to read them all?" They agreed the timing and found a date for the prize giving that suited them both. With that fixed, Margaret set out the rules for the competition and set a deadline date for entries, she prepared announcement notices and leaflets designed to encourage entries, and spoke to Alice Carter at the local paper who promised that they would run a story about the announcement and the prize giving. There was also work to do to put an announcement on the library web site and make sure that various social media also had details; she was not great at social media and roped in a better informed colleague to help with that. She also spoke directly to several contacts the library had in local schools. When she reckoned it was all set she requested a meeting with Philip and they sat down together in his small office.

"How shall we do this? I want you to approve everything I have planned and I thought it might be best to run through it chronologically. Does that sound okay?"

"Yes, fine, that seems sensible, let's hear it." One of the things she liked best about her boss was that he was prepared to listen. She went through the details, stage by stage, describing what she planned and showing him things like drafts of the announcement leaflets and posters.

"Looks good, what about costs, you know we can't afford too much."

"Yes, I do know that." The grinned at each other, both well aware that costs were a regular consideration in everything that the library did.

"Anyway I have worked out a rough budget, it's not too much, mainly some print and we can do that in-house. Eve Watson does not want a fee, she's pleased to help us and I've put her picture and an image of one of her book covers on the announcements so she will get some publicity from the event. I thought we might give her some flowers at the prize giving. A couple of businesses in the High Street have agreed to subsidize the prizes. So I think the overall cost is manageable. Look." She passed an A4 sheet across the desk to him. Philip scanned it with care, asked if he could keep the figures and was told the copy was for him.

"I think that's all fine. The only thing that's unclear is exactly what will happen on the day. Eve Watson needs to speak of course, but we will need a library introduction, we should host the event so to speak. Right?" Philip looked at her expectantly.

"Yes, of course, I had assumed you would want to introduce at the start."

"No. No, it's your event, I think it makes better sense for you to do it. You will know all the details, you'll have seen it through. Not too short, not too long, some thanks and a plug for the library. If you need to run any ideas about it past me just ask, but I am sure you can do it perfectly well." Margaret expressed surprise, the thought made her somewhat apprehensive, but she was also keen to rise to the occasion. She reckoned that she would cope. Everything was set, the meeting ended and they both went back to their other duties.

"Thanks, Margaret, I'm glad it's all in good hands," said Philip as she left his office.

Once the announcement of the competition was made, entries started to come in after a week or two, Margaret read them all and created a file as the numbers crept up pretty well. Inevitably there were some shockers, both in terms of the writing and of the presentation – several contained some bizarre spellings (perhaps showing that spell checkers are definitely not a cure all) and one featured some surprisingly rude words. Too rude Margaret thought. However, when the closing date for entries arrived Margaret screened a few out as non-starters and then reckoned she had a good batch to pass on to her chosen judge. She had arranged for Eve Watson to pick them up; Margaret did not want them lost in the post or for her judge to have to print them all out if they were sent by email. The library called on numbers of people for favours to support their cause and always wanted to make it as easy as possible for any volunteer to do their bit. Once the entries had been handed over she had only to wait for a decision and think about the details of the prize giving day.

*

A couple of weeks later Margaret was busy in the library answering a question from a member, a woman with a seven or eight year old son in tow.

"He wants another book like one he particularly liked recently, but he can't remember the title... or the author," she said with a kind of what-can-you-do shrug. Margaret was well used to such questions, the words "I'm afraid I can't remember..." started many a conversation with library members, and she asked him what he did remember.

"It had a blue cover," said the boy with an air that saying so might solve everything.

"And, anything else that might help?" The boy screwed up his face in exaggerated concentration and thought for a moment"

"It had time travel in the title, and animals, it was funny, but an adventure too. If there are more by that author then that's what I want next... please?" Margaret, like everyone in the library was all geared up to encourage their regular visitors, especially children and, on this occasion, she thought she knew the right answer.

"Was the animal a hamster?"

"Oh, yes."

"Was it called *Time travelling with a hamster?*"

"Yes, yes, that's it. See Mum I told you we should ask." He looked up at her as he spoke.

"In that case it's written by Ross Welford and I think you will find another of his on the shelf under that name, it's called

"*What not to do if you become invisible*". His books are very popular, now do you know where to look?" This got a brief yes as he turned and rushed off to the children's section, while the mother offered her thanks and hurried after him. Before Margaret could do anything else she was called to the telephone. It was Eve Watson.

"Hello Margaret. I have to say judging this competition of yours has been fun. A fair number of the entries are really good, it's great to see kids doing this sort of thing, isn't it?" Margaret agreed and let her continue.

"I don't have the names of entrants of course, you gave each of them a reference number as you know, but I have two clear winners, numbers 28 and 29 – consecutive numbers. We agreed on two best, didn't we, rather than a first and second? Can I do anything else, do you want the entries sent back?"

"No, by all means hang onto them, I have copies. And thanks so much, nothing more for you to do, well not until the prize giving – I will be in touch later about arrangements on the day, I look forward to seeing you again then. Now I can't wait to look up and read the winners' entries. Thanks again, you're a star." She wrote 28 and 29 on a notepad and thought everything was now pretty much organised to make the event go smoothly. But not everything is so predictable.

CHAPTER SIX

A proper story

"Get on with it then."

Rude. Bob is always so abrupt, but I guess I should be well used to it by now. What does the dictionary say about abrupt. "Sudden and unexpected", well his instructions may be sudden but his rudeness is never unexpected. The word abrupt is also defined as "curt" and frankly that sounds more like it. He is always curt, but then he is the editor: 'Bob Norton. Editor' it says on his door, a painted sign to which has been added a simple face on the letter O of Bob. I sometimes wonder how many of my colleagues have noticed my handiwork, no one has ever said anything. A while ago in my head I started to refer to him as Smaug, the evil dragon in Tolkien's book "The Hobbit". As a trainee reporter it seems that he regards me as the lowest of the low.

I close the door as I come out of his office with somewhat more force than is necessary and revel in the satisfying thump it makes. I go to get on with it as he says; it is just a phone call. This is a career stage that one has to put up with, I guess, it isn't easy to get into journalism and a spell on a local paper is a tried and tested first step and can provide a route to better things in the long term. I am never allowed to forget how lucky I am to be paid to write anything at all, but at this stage of my career, barely six months in, I am happy to be giving it a go and am pleased to see even the simplest item appear in the paper with a by-line – my name, "By Alice Carter" – appearing in print along with the feature. I like it best when my name appears at the top of an article, believing that this will be seen by someone even if they don't read to the end of the item. I am learning a great deal and, for all I moan about him, Smaug did give me the job, and it's one that is certainly enjoyable for much of the time. I have contemporaries from university who are still packing parcels in some dreary warehouse.

I look at my notebook and remind myself what it is I have to 'get on with', as he always puts it, today. Some of the things are regular or minor items, like writing up the announcement of a local fete. However, some others have possibilities, sometimes I get to put things on my list that have more significance and might actually turn into a story of some substance. I wonder about the current crop: I have to telephone James Kent. This is what Smaug's last chaser was about. Kent is the Managing Director of the international giant Demonaxx Pharmaceuticals and lives in the local area. His company is taking a lot of flak because their drug Demoniximol, having been proved to be very successful in the treatment of certain kinds of cancer, is currently being offered for sale at such a high price that it cannot be approved for general use in the NHS. The company is busy fighting off attacks from press, public and an action group formed specially to try to affect a change and get the drug made widely available. The row seems ironic as the company takes its name from the Greek philosopher, Demonaxx, who throughout his long life was more than anything renowned for being a peacemaker. The core issue is a national story of course, but we would like to get some sort of statement from him for the Maldon Express as he's a local resident. Smaug only sees that as a small story, and hence one he is prepared to leave to little old me.

Despite having been unsuccessful on several previous occasions, I reach for the phone and dial Demonaxx's number again. I have found that a high degree of persistence seems to be one of my job's main requirements.

"Hello, may I speak with James Kent please?" To date I have always been very polite to them, although in my view they are bunch of money grabbing anti-social clowns charging so much for what is billed as a life saver from which very few people will therefore benefit. I am put through to his office, but that much I have achieved before.

"Who's calling?" I am pretty sure that it is the same person who always answers and that they recognise my voice now. She sounds bored and uninterested, or maybe the tone is just designed to be off putting, but I introduce myself anyway.

"It's Alice Carter from the Maldon Express, look I'll only keep Mr Kent a minute… please."

"You again."

"Yes that's right, me again."

"I know you're only doing your job Ms Carter but I'm afraid he is adamant, I am not to put you through." I try one quick question.

"Okay, if he won't talk to me can *you* tell me if he has spoken to anyone from CvC?" Cure versus Cost is the action group that has been leading the charge on the matter, and getting pretty good press coverage for their efforts too.

"No, Ms Carter, I can't." She always calls me Ms Carter, very formal, and as usual she does not wait for me to say more but simply ends the call. I listen for a moment to the dialling tone and draw a stroke across the final four lines on my note about Demonaxx to make a gate; that makes three gates, fifteen calls to date and I know Smaug will want me to call again tomorrow, especially as the most recent rumour is that Kent has been getting death threats amongst the protests. Now it really would be a story for us if he was killed at his home in Maldon. No, that's an unworthy thought I suppose – now what's next?

*

In the months running up to Christmas the local library has been running a story writing competition for children, I wrote a story about its announcement, and there is going to be an event set up before long to award the prizes. The competition is being judged by a local writer of children's' books. That all seems to make it a reasonable and worthwhile story, certainly I am in favour of anything that promotes reading and writing for kids. I need to speak to the librarian who has already said I may "call in anytime we are open".

"I'm off to the library, be back soon." I shout to Becky, Smaug's secretary, who also acts as our receptionist and sits at the front of the open plan office in which I inhabit my small cubicle. I grab my anorak and head for the door. Five minutes down the road and I cut through a pedestrian walkway leading off the High Street and running alongside the food store Iceland towards one of the town's car parks and am soon in the library alongside it. I go to the main desk.

"Can I speak to Philip Marchington for a moment please? I'm Alice Carter from the Maldon Express." I like libraries and look around me as I wait while someone summons him. Some books sit on a trolley not far away with a "Sale" notice on them; I resolve to check that out before I leave, I can never resist a bargain book.

"Hello there Alice." I look round to see Philip Marchington smiling at me. He is as enthusiastic a library manager as you could hope to imagine and is always helpful. We have crossed paths briefly a few times over my six months with the paper. I explain I want to get a bit of background before the event announcing the competition results takes place and am referred on.

"Margaret has been handling all of that, it's her day. I'll get her for you and you can have a word, just hang on a sec." Philip disappears into the back and I recall him previously describing Margaret as a sort of protégé. Though she's the youngest member of the library team he thinks she is good and wants to "bring her along" as he put it. A few minutes later I am sitting with Margaret in the magazine area. This is busiest in the cold weather when people with little to do come into the warm for a breather. At the moment there is only a handful of people there, one appears to be doing serious work making extensive notes and with a large reference book in front of them, but most are reading newspapers and magazines. Margaret has found us a corner. She has even organised me a cup of coffee. She is about my age, in her early twenties, and we chat agreeably. I reckon we probably have a fair bit in common.

"The competition is all about getting publicity for the library and especially in context of kids," she says. "You know how keen Philip is to encourage reading. We all are." She describes the main details of how the occasion will go and ends up saying: "I think we will have a good turnout, your report last week drew attention to it and all the local schools have been very supportive. I think we will find we get a fair number of people attending on the day."

"Are you to do the introductions?"

"Yes, well, when I started here that kind of thing used to terrify me, but Philip got me visiting schools, you know doing readings for the children, now I've kind of got used to it. Well, sort of, though I assumed that Philip would do the honours on this occasion. But he insisted I do it; I still have to work out what to say."

"Well, reminds me of the old saying: if you don't strike oil in the first five minutes, stop boring. I'll certainly be there, so see you then." I am not sure I would like to have to do that kind of thing, I like to think that I'm good with words, but I'm much happier putting them down on paper. Despite that I make the quip and get a smile back, I hope she didn't think I was being rude. I reckon she will cope well enough.

I thank her, we part company and I move to head back to the office, pausing on the way to check the sale trolley which I pass on the way. I can't resist a copy of the late Keith Waterhouse's book *On Newspaper Style*; he was a wonderful writer and I am sure any lessons this has for me will be put over with some humour. I pay at the desk, pop it in my bag and move on. The prize presentation should make a nice story, not so important that old Smaug will want someone more senior on it, but a substantial enough piece for me to enjoy having my name on. I hope I'll have written so much in due course that I'll grow out of it, but for the moment a copy of everything I write that goes in the paper, byline or not, I put in a special scrapbook. My mother bought it for me when I got the job and at first I thought it was rather pretentious, though I did I thank her for it. Now I tell myself that such a record may be useful one day and that it's not just for bragging purposes; I imagine this piece to be the next to be included.

Back at my desk I make a telephone call to the competition judge, thinking that she might let me in on the name of the winners up front. No chance: "On the day," she says. "Only on the day." I fancy I can almost feel her bristling at the very idea as she speaks and there seems no point in pushing the issue. I ask her if she will have a word with me on the day, to which she happily agrees, say I look forward to meeting her at the prize giving and hang up. There's a shout from the doorway of the Editor's office: "Alice, I need our expert on lost dogs?" Another one. Oh joy.

One day I need to get a proper story to write. I live in hopes.

CHAPTER SEVEN
I don't mean to be rude

I drive past James Kent's home. He lives in a large rather grand house set well back from the road in Wickham Bishops. This is a village two or three miles outside Maldon on the way to Witham, it's a place that has always seemed to me to have a good few more than its fair share of large expensive houses. I know little about the place other than that its house prices are high. In part that's because it is so well situated for commuting to London from the station in nearby Witham, it's a place that goes way back and was listed in the Doomsday Book, though at that time it went under the name of Wicham. It's remarkable the facts that being a reporter sees you squirrelling away.

Anyway, today's big surprise: James Kent has finally agreed to see me, the cold fish in his office had new instructions and had been told to fix it, though I couldn't persuade her to get him to see me at his home. So I drive past his large and imposing house and get the train to London. My appointment is set for 9.00 a.m. It was take it or leave it so I am travelling in the morning rush hour, and have a trip that will take half a day when it could have been done so much more simply. The train is packed; probably extra packed as it is not long now till Christmas and shoppers are mixing with commuters. I stand clutching a metal pole, swaying about somewhat as I am unaccustomed to the process of rush hour commuting. When I do go to London on the train, and it's not so often that I do, I normally go later in the day and get a lower fare - and a seat. I feel pretty sure James Kent opted for a 9 a.m. appointment to maximise my inconvenience; I am coming to dislike him even more. After a forty minute train journey and a short trip on the Underground I arrive.

The office is in a tall glass, marble and stainless steel block close to Canary Wharf in London's Docklands. The atrium-style reception area makes me think of rich architects and ego trips. There's a fountain for goodness sake, surely always a sign that a company is rather too introspective, there's also a great deal of marble, I see more and more of it as I go deeper into the building.

"Good morning, I've an appointment with James Kent," I say, making an effort to speak in a cheerful, business like, tone.

Although she is sitting down behind a huge desk the receptionist still manages to look down her nose at me. She indicates a seat and tells me to wait. The seat is modern in the extreme, but very uncomfortable, a triumph of style over practicality, and it's a full half an hour past nine before Kent's secretary comes to collect me. She offers no apology. Now, after rising up many floors in a glass sided lift that almost induces vertigo as it travels up the outside of the building, I am sitting in his office. He offers a brief "Morning" and points to a chair opposite his desk and I sit down; more comfortably this time. He looks me up and down. I doubt he's assessing any degree of attractiveness I may possess, my unruly and naturally curly hair is doubtless even more unruly after my journey, and I remain swaddled in a rather old anorak, one which even a desperate charity shop might well reject but which I needed for the journey on a cold morning. I push my oversized horn rimmed glasses up my nose and stare back at him. He looks as if he is inspecting something irrelevant and a little unpleasant. I say nothing, but smile just a little, exposing the slight but noticeable gap between my front teeth, and stare on, waiting for him to speak. I may be scruffy by his reckoning, but I am not to be put off. I represent the power of the press; after all, that nice Mrs McKeith got her dog back after I reported the circumstances of its disappearance. He speaks again.

"I don't mean to be rude," he says. Not a good start, it almost certainly means that he intends to be precisely that. "But I'm very busy. I suppose a small piece in the local paper would do no harm. I have prepared you a short statement and will allow you to quote that."

He passes me a sheet of paper with a considered air of finality.

"I had hoped to ask you some questions," I retort. I had struggled to scribble some down in my notebook as the train had lurched unpredictably on its way to London. The notebook sits open in front of me and I clutch my smart Cross pen, a roller ball and another present from my mother. She was pleased and proud that I got the job, but also, I suspect, pleased to get me out of the house and wanting to see me "stand on my own feet", as she put it, which I suspect meant things like eating lots of fruit and veg, budgeting sensibly and doing my own washing. She sometimes seems to forget that I spent three years fending for myself at university. Kent looks pointedly at what is clearly an expensive watch and decides to allow me a moment more.

"Like what?"

I am clearly going to get only a few brief minutes at best so I cut straight to what seems to me to be the chase.

"This refusal to set a reasonable price for Demoniximol doesn't seem to be making you many friends, witness the Cure versus Cost protest group that's been set up. Tell me, is it true that recently you've had death threats?"

"No, that's not true." His reply comes quickly, then he pauses, steepling his hands together in front of him, and I fear I am on my way out. But after a moment he does continue.

"No, not death threats, though I have to admit that complaints have made a certain amount of work." He indicates a ragged six inch high stack of papers on the corner of his desk, somewhere that I can imagine each new complaint being tossed onto and quickly forgotten. The desk is so huge that the corner, and the stack of papers on it, is way out of his reach. I lean forward a little and pick up the top dozen or so sheets. I open my mouth to speak, but before I can suggest it might be useful to see the kind of thing involved, this gets an immediate reaction.

"No." His voice is loud to the point of being better called shrill. It sounds almost funny coming from the mouth of someone so... conventional: grey suit, silk tie, well-tended hair, steel framed spectacles, the first tiny touch of grey at his temples – he's the picture of respectability. And power.

"No. How dare you? Put those back at once."

My hand jerks in response to his sudden utterance and I drop the sheets I am holding on the floor where they spread out sliding across a carpet with sufficiently thick pile to bury any small items dropped from his massive desk forever. I apologise for my mistake as I bend to pick them up, shuffling them together before putting them back on top of the appropriate heap on his desk. The dictionary will tell us that fortuitous does not, as many people believe, mean something lucky, it means something happening accidental or by chance. This was not a fortuitous event.

"Right, that's enough. You should leave and I would be grateful if you would see there is no more of this constant phoning. A statement will be issued to the press if anything changes, for the moment you have my comment, please leave it at that." I do not rate my chances of overcoming the degree of firmness now sounding in his voice. He is angry and, more relevant, he is adamant, but I have one more try.

"As this is for the local paper, and things are obviously hectic and difficult, can you tell me how all this affects your family and home life?"

"There is always something presenting a challenge in a big job like this, but I don't see how that is relevant. Enough now." I think by 'big' he means important. It seems that there is no more to be done for the moment.

"Okay, I'll be going. I will make a point of mentioning how helpful you have been."

Okay, not my finest hour perhaps, but I couldn't stop myself from saying something sarcastic. I find myself liking James Kent less and less.

I make my way back to Liverpool Street, check the time of the next train to Witham, and phone Becky to tell her when I will be back in the office. I have time for an over-priced coffee and sit on a cold and uncomfortable seat outside a café on the platform and look at Kent's statement. It does not surprise me that it's short and bland:

> *Demoniximol is the result of years of expensive research by top scientists… it represents a major breakthrough… clinical trials now completed show it will extend and save many lives… there are no significant adverse side effects… the company, indeed, the pharmaceutical industry of which it is a part, is a success story within the economy… a significant exporter… Demonaxx is an enterprise run to improve the lot of mankind… blah, blah, blah… negotiations with the NHS are continuing to make this important drug more widely available.*

Yeah, right. Even though I believe this is just trying to disguise a period of excess profit making, there is nothing there to help me create the story of the week, but I already have a handful of facts about the man, where he lives of course, his having a wife and children, so, even without mention of profiteering I can probably write a useful piece. After all the key thing I can now add in is something genuinely new about those "complaints" I saw. Most were letters, presumably making a case for lowering the price of the drug, and three or four of them appeared to be from the same person, though they had no name and address on them. I saw that one was signed: outraged and concerned. But one sheet was definitely different. It was typed, I saw only a few short sentences, its letters were sizeable, perhaps in 26 point type. I only glimpsed two phrases: Action will now be taken to make you pay, and: You have been warned. I didn't see the word death, but this was clearly and most definitely a threat and could and would be described as such. Now that is news and hopefully my grumpy editor will see it as worth my having made a lengthy trip to London involving the cost of a full price rail ticket. I get a seat on my return journey and can make a few notes as I head back towards the office.

*

Back in the office at my computer I open a new document and start typing. I put together about 400 words, headed by the words "Controversy sees local top industrialist threatened", email it to Smaug and wait for a response. His shout comes about five minutes later.

"Alice, John, get in here." John Roberts is a few years older than me, and certainly more senior, he's been in the post for about three years and must be around thirty now. I think he was born middle aged and he always wears a brown cord jacket with elbow patches very like the one that my university tutor always wore, and he must have been ninety. He's pleasant enough in his way, and has been quite helpful to me, but I hate that he gets jobs I would like for myself. We go into the Editor's office – Smaug's lair. John leads the way in and plonks himself in the only empty chair, I contemplate moving a bundle of papers off the only other one but settle for leaning against the doorway, as always with my trusty notebook in hand.

"This will do for the next edition, Alice." My 400 words seems to have passed muster. "Given what you discovered, we need to see if we can sell a piece about the threats to a national paper. John you know the procedure, can you do that? You know how much such things help our budget. Liaise together as necessary." No surprise there, John gets to follow it up and I don't even get a proper thank you for providing some real and important news: confirmation that Kent's company has received threats. We leave the office and I head back to my cubicle. If John is successful, then I don't doubt that James Kent will never speak to me again. I call across the room to John.

"If you get anything fixed, John, do let me know. I should reword the last bit of my piece if the fact that there have been threats has been in the nationals before this week's Express comes out." He agrees to do so. Six months ago I would have said "hits the streets" but in my first week I learnt never to say anything like that.

I think back to my meeting with James Kent. The man seemed insufferable. The dictionary says that means "intolerable – unbearable, arrogant or conceited"; that seems about right to me. But I have little experience of titans of industry, maybe being one such acts to make you hard and I am being hard on him. Maybe. I am sure he is busy, it's doubtless a taxing, pressurised and important job being the head of such a large organisation. I wonder what he's like at home, I know he has a wife and children. Perhaps they love him.

CHAPTER EIGHT

An easy task

He now knew what he wanted to do, after lengthy head scratching and the rejection of a dozen still born plans the idea had come to him in a flash one morning and he found only a little research had been necessary to persuade himself that it was a real possibility. He had then worked through the details many times, he could find no holes and was sure he could make it work. It needed a suitable place and he had set out to find one. The house seemed to lend itself to the task. It was detached and stood at the very end of a quiet cul-de-sac. The houses along either side of the road were newer, and there was space between the house he planned to use and them, the ugly bulk of an electricity substation distancing the houses on one side and a vacant plot, an overgrown patch with a foundation of some long gone building on it, and yet to be built on again, doing the same on the other.

The house itself was undistinguished and somewhat run down, a rough drive replete with weeds ran alongside the house and ended at a garage round the back. Out of sight. He had first seen the place online, looked at it from the outside, then telephoned the number on an estate agent's "For Sale/Let" board posted at the front and been told that the house was in fact sold. A little more chatter had unearthed the information that it was to be extended and totally renovated in a one off development project that would see it upgraded and increased in size. On the pretext that he wanted to pick the brains of the new owner about development he got their name and contact details from the agent. He had negotiated on the phone and a slightly over generous cash payment, pushed through a letterbox, had finalised a few weeks' rental deal for him. He had spun them a tale about an unplanned delay on a house purchase leaving him needing accommodation to bridge the gap and the developer had been only too eager to get a little cash towards the work he was planning to do on the house. The keys were left under a stone in the garden and they never even met.

The spare bedroom he had prepared for his purposes was at the rear of the house, and outside at the back, beyond the small neglected garden there was a stretch of wasteland so overgrown no one appeared to ever battle through its veritable jungle of tall brambles and nettles. One day no doubt it would be built on. Effectively it meant that the bedroom was completely protected from view.

Before his other preparations were made he had switched on a portable radio in the bedroom and turned it up to its loudest setting and then walked around outside. It demonstrated that no one in the nearby houses would be able to hear anything if there was shouting. Anyway it would not be for long, all his arrangements had been made with that important assumption in mind and his sound check reassured him all would be well on that score.

His first illegal act, a comparatively mild one, was undertaken at night.

His plan needed a car and he did not want to risk his own vehicle being recognised. He couldn't steal a car, not least because he wouldn't know how to do that, so he needed false number plates for his own. In the end, after a little time checking it out, it proved an easy task. It was not the same make as his own car but he had found something of similar age to it parked in the far recesses of the car park behind the Maldon "Prom", the stretch of open space alongside Maldon's River Blackwater, where the wide estuary narrowed into the more modest stream that flowed through the town. The car was not only clamped but had seemed to have been clamped for days, a warning notice stuck to its windscreen gave the date and warned of increasing penalties for inaction; he had revisited it several times to check that it had not been moved. Maybe the owner was sick, who knew? It had been a simple matter to go there in the dead of night, unscrew its number plates, wrap them in an old table cloth and carry them to his own car which he had parked some distance away down the road. No closed circuit television had been apparent nearby, though he had taken care to wear a cap pulled low over his eyes and had wrapped a scarf around his face. He wore gloves. It had been a cold night and he had been sure that no one was about to notice him.

A moment online had secured him information that had allowed him to leave an envelope containing a short note under the car's windscreen. He would fix the stolen plates to his own car out of sight in his garage later. As each part of his preparations was completed he became more confident of the viability of his plan overall. If all went well he felt that both of his two objectives could be achieved safely. Despite one aspect he would have preferred to be different, he had convinced himself that what he would achieve, what circumstances had prompted him to feel he must achieve, made the results and the up-front costs he had incurred worth what risks were involved.

For the moment he went back to his own home, put the number plates in the garage and returned to a wrapping job that saw a small pile of gift wrapped items in the corner of the living room increase in size. Enough, another small bit of the jigsaw was complete.

CHAPTER NINE
Welcome to you all

"Hi, Alice, glad you could come." Margaret welcomes me in as I arrive at the library on the day of the children's writing competition prize announcement. I had arranged to arrive a little time ahead of the formal start so I find the library currently just going on quietly about its normal business. I like libraries. Correction, I love them and am very much in favour of them, it's such a shame that recent government cut backs have threatened them in various ways, at worst for some with closure. The town of Maldon is very lucky to have a good one, headed up by someone who is an advocate for books, reading and especially for children learning to read and enjoying what they are then able to read. For some, like me, a good start with books produces a lifetime's habit. I have always been told that I read early and have clear memories of struggling to get up the steps to the mobile library van that stopped nearby because my legs were still too short to mount them easily. When I moved to Maldon one of the first things I did was to join the library. My mind's wandering, I realise that Margaret is still talking and I tune back in.

"We've got a little while to go, come and meet our judge, I've got us some biscuits to go with a cuppa." I follow her into the back premises and find Eve Watson sitting at a table with a plate of biscuits in front of her and a mug of coffee in her hand. We introduce ourselves and I find she isn't frosty in the least as I judged her to be when we spoke on the phone, rather she is a smartly dressed woman of maybe forty or so years and looks fiercely intelligent. So I forgive her at once for refusing me advance information. Since I had first heard that she was the judge I had looked her up and borrowed one of her books from the library. It seemed very good, especially for its target audience of eight to ten year olds, though I'm not sure that I can remember exactly the kind of thing I read that far back. Margaret gives me a mug and we all exchange a few pleasantries, mainly about Eve's writing, then finally get down to business.

"So what's the plan?" Cuppa nearly finished I addressed this question to Margaret who I know has organised the whole project.

"Well, the kids should be here in about half an hour. Julie and Jake. I asked them to arrive early so that they have a moment to get used to the idea, though they both come to the library regularly so they are well used to the place. Then, hopefully, when we formally start there will be an audience of some sort assembled, there will be a short introduction following which Eve takes over and will say a little about the judging process and the winning entries. The kids were asked if they wanted to read their stories out loud – the word limit was sufficiently few so that doing so is possible without the process taking too long - and both were enthusiastic to do it; I'm pleased about that, though Eve has a printed copy too and can take over if either of them should become tongue tied."

"How old are they?" Wondering about their intention to read aloud, I interrupt her.

"Ten and eight," she replied. "The top age limit for competition entrants was eleven."

"What's Philip going to say to start things off?" I wondered what role the head of the library would have.

"Not Philip actually, he'll be there, of course, but if you remember he's insisted on leaving it all to me, though, now I think about it, he'll take some photos. I'll just take a minute or two to link the competition to our work as a library and introduce our judge." Margaret smiles at Eve and I kick myself for not remembering about the introduction. I apologise. I do reckon that's the sort of boss to have though, an active delegator. I think of Smaug shouting clipped instructions from inside his lair and making it clear I should expect little and toe the line, though this little story at least is all mine and I am grateful for that. The event does not rate a photographer as well as a reporter, Smaug had expected me to take some shots on my phone, I reckon I'll leave that to Philip now and get copies from him after the event. I make a mental note to ask him about it later.

"Okay, let's get out front, I want us to be there when the children arrive." Margaret leads the way back to the main library area, which is busier now that more people are arriving. As we move to where a microphone is set up in the far corner, what is clearly a school group comes in. I reckon many from the winner's classes must be here. There are four adults, teachers or parents I assume, and about thirty kids who flow around the area pushing a blast of noisy chatter in front of them. I lose sight of Margaret for the moment, but now she reappears, coming towards me with two grinning children in tow, both looking as if they are clearly excited about what's to come, and with them is a woman who I assume is their mother.

"This is our proud mother, Elizabeth Kent. Alice Carter and Eve Watson." Elizabeth Kent is a slim woman I judge to be in her late forties and I address her as she steps towards us.

"Hello, I'm Alice Carter, I'll be writing all about the event for the Maldon Express." She says a brief hello and we shake hands, then as she turns to speak to Eve, I greet the children who are, after all, today's star players.

"And you must be Julie and Jake. The heroes of the hour. Well done to you both. May I have a word with you both when the formalities are over?" They both nod their heads enthusiastically, then quickly return to scanning the room taking everything in; it's a big day for them.

"Will we be in the paper?" asks Julie, who is clearly the younger. Both the children are smartly turned out for the event. Jake is wearing a jacket, though not a tie, and Julie is in a russet coloured corduroy dress, a matching band holding her shoulder length blond hair back in a ponytail. They seem like nice kids, though what would I know? They may run riot at home. Probably do. They clearly have an abundance of energy.

"I can't promise the front page, but you will certainly be in there." I have no great experience of children of this age, but I give them what I hope is an encouraging smile and wish them well.

The key players move into a group around the microphone, where some chairs are laid out in a semi-circle, Margaret steps up to it and onto a small kitchen stool so that she is properly visible to what is now a reasonable crowd of both adults and children. The initial publicity seems to have worked well. A loud speaker sits atop a pole on a tripod off to her right. Most people are standing, there being way more people present than there are chairs in the library. Amongst the children that have joined the throng some look round inquisitively as if unfamiliar with the place. That's one of the things that Philip and Margaret want: for this sort of event to provide an introduction for some new visitors. Regular users who happen to have found themselves in the library as the event unfolds are pausing to see what is going on, and a mix of people are all forming a semi-circle around the microphone. All in all the central area is pretty much filled, there are people young and old, I imagine some are friends and family of the winners, others may just have seen the notices in the library about the event or read about it in my initial announcement in the paper. A variety of people are there, most wearing coats, though one is in a Father Christmas outfit, a few have kept hats on (it is cold outside) and I imagine there is a wide list of reasons for their presence.

"Good morning everyone and welcome to you all," Margaret taps the microphone, three sharp taps before she speaks, and the chatter dies away. I switch on my recorder. She welcomes everyone, introduces Eve Watson, thanking her and giving her books a nice plug as she does so, and then introduces the children. She takes a few minutes to add a good plug for the library and the power and importance of books and stories. Not too short, not too long, she's done well. I think I see a smile cross Philip's face as she hands over to Eve. He's standing well back and it seems to me that he really is a good boss.

Eve does an excellent job too. She starts by saying how well supported the competition has been.

"Good morning everyone, we received lots of entries, many of them very good – well done to all who entered. We wanted to pick winners that were good stories: clever, interesting, exciting or intriguing and which were also well written. Two entries stood out on this basis and our two winners surprised us by being brother and sister." She explains that judging took place with entries only identified by a reference number, so as she read them she had had no idea even if a particular story she was reading was from a boy or a girl or what age they might be. She congratulates Jake and Julie profusely, then continues.

"Now, stand by for a treat everyone: our winners have agreed to read their stories to you, now who's going to go first?" There are just two winners, not a first and second, and three more kids are mentioned as "highly recommended" and will receive a Book Token each in due course. The microphone is lowered, the children read well and their stories are good, I think. Jake's is my favourite. He tells of a boy waking up on Christmas Eve and finding Father Christmas in his room, this of course surprises him, but they talk and Father Christmas suggests he opens one of his presents – a long thin package that, once unwrapped, turns out to be a machine gun. Just as the appalled boy is responding: "You can't give me that" and being told: "It's not a problem there's an operating manual with it" – he wakes up and finds it's all been just a dream. On Christmas morning, after breakfast, the story ends with him finding that the first real present he opens from under the Christmas tree is – a machine gun! Delightfully surreal. What kind of imagination produces that? Julie has also written something linked to Christmas, a story that starts with a cracking first line: The saddest thing I can imagine is that if every day in the year was Christmas Day, but there was no Santa Claus. Each receive a round of applause after their reading, something that allows them to demonstrate that you can look both embarrassed and delighted all at the same time, though I'm sure that delight wins. Eve hands over their prizes and they both say a polite thank you.

Formalities over, the kids open their prizes – an envelope containing a £20 Book Token and a watch for each of them. Jake can't wait, he tears open the box and straps his new watch on his left wrist. It's bright orange and looks to me like something an astronaut might wear to help pilot the space shuttle. He holds his arm outstretched for a moment and mouths a wow sound.

As the room returns to an untidy chattering crowd I need to get quotes from the key players, first the judge: "I found the overall high standard of entries was surprising and pleasing, and the winners produced something both quirky, fun and well written. Well done Jake and Julie – and well done to our lovely library for organising all of this." Eve gives me something spot on for the piece I will write later. I have my phone's recorder switched on but also scribble her words in my notebook to be safe.

"It's a pleasure to do this sort of thing, I reckon enthusing our young library members about reading and writing is one of the most important things a library can do." That's great Philip, and will suit well too. I thank him for his comment and commend him for the whole idea and event. Margaret will get mentioned as the person organising and introducing the event: I am sure that I can quote some of what she said too.

"It's what we are here for," he says in a way that suggests he really does see it as a key part of the job.

Elizabeth Kent seems quite overcome. "I'm just so very proud," she says, just repeating the same words when I ask her to say more.

"Is the children's father here?" I ask.

"No my husband couldn't get away from work, it's a busy time." Her voice tails off. I wonder if that's a common situation for her.

"That's a shame, but I'm sure he's just as proud of them as you are. They did do really well, I think. Do you mind if I ask, do you live in Maldon? That's something that ought to go in the article."

"We're in Wickham Bishops." Hmm, I wonder some more. I very much think I have met this particular Mr Kent quite recently and, if that is the case, then I understand exactly why he's too busy to be here this morning and it's nothing to do with the festive season. Elizabeth Kent thanks Philip, Margaret and Eve for their part in the whole event and is then set to move on. She glances at her watch.

"I must find the kids, our time will be up in the car park before you know it."

"Yes, let's do that, I'd like to collect some words from them to quote in the paper too, before you all go. Where have they got to?" We look around the room, the group is thinning out now the event is over, it should be easy to spot people, but for the moment we can't see the kids anywhere.

CHAPTER TEN
Another prize

He reckoned everything was in place and had arrived at the library just five minutes before the prize giving was due to start, he was pleased to see there was quite a number of people in the room. Adults and children, some no doubt attending specifically for the event, others regular library users. A reasonable crowd would help. Though his costume made him stand out in some respects, it was also anonymous and he felt secure so dressed in the crowd. No one would think a Father Christmas suit odd at this time of year. His car, now displaying the stolen number plates, was parked outside close to the library entrance. It was on a yellow line, but he had put a bold sign in the windscreen saying: "Delivering to Library" and it was blocking nothing. You occasionally saw a traffic warden round about, certainly the nearby car park was checked regularly for those overstaying their allotted time or not paying at all, but on a chilly December morning he reckoned his car would be left unmolested for a while. It was one small uncontrollable element in his plan, but represented only a tiny risk he thought.

He knew the Kent kids would be there and their presence provided the perfect opportunity and fitted his plan well. Originally he had thought to lure one of the children away from the school playground. He had felt that was possible using the Father Christmas disguise he had on now, but that was always going to be a risky method, especially with so many other curious children about wondering why one of them was suddenly not returning to lessons. Then a chance event had changed everything and led to a revision to his plan, to what he regarded as an improvement.

It had started a few days earlier when he had discovered by accident that they had won the competition. He had been in the library, returning a book, and he had overheard one of the staff talking about the event. "I must phone Mrs Kent and let her know the timing for the kids' writing prize giving." The young woman had said that much clearly before moving out of earshot and he had already read about the writing competition and it seemed natural it was that being referred to. Could it be the very same Kent family he wanted? He had reckoned that the winner would have had been told well ahead of time that they had won to be sure they would be there for the prize giving, and surely the word would soon go round the school. Arriving at the school residents of Wickham Bishops were most likely to use at 8.3o the next morning he had got the winners' names confirmed from the third kid he asked amongst those hanging about just before going into school. A little more checking soon showed that it was his Mr Kent who was the father. Julie and Jake were his children. His intention had been to take one of them, but now he was settled on a plan he couldn't see a way of separating them without it causing additional risk; one would surely miss the other very quickly. He was sure his plan would still work with two of them, though it had first necessitated some additional shopping.

He was brought out of his thoughts by the sound of three sharp taps on the microphone. One of the Library staff, a young woman, was getting the formalities under way and the audience became still and focussed on what was happening, though, with a good many kids in the room, a bit of fidgeting continued along with the occasional "Shush" or "Keep still" voiced by a parent or teacher. He half listened and, when it became clear that the children were to read their stories out loud, he realised that the event would last a little longer than he had originally anticipated. There were clearly still a few more minutes to go, so he slipped over to the library entrance to check his car was still parked safely. His plan would likely survive being given a ticket without a problem, but clamping would be the end of it. He looked around outside and was relieved to see no warden was in sight; indeed his car was now fronting a row of three other illegally parked cars. He returned to the main room to find closing remarks being made and thanks being given to all those involved. As he watched the lady judge was presented with a bouquet of flowers and the event was at an end.

As the final applause died away everyone began moving about, every child in the room seemed to be weaving in and out of the crowd in every random direction possible and after a minute or two he saw Julie and Jake emerge nearby and seemingly about to head right past him on the way to a table on which drinks were laid out, just squash and biscuits, no alcohol at this time of the morning or on limited library budgets.

"Well done you two," he said and the children stopped in front of him. They may have wondered why he was speaking to them, but there was no surprise at seeing a Father Christmas anywhere at this time of year.

"Good stories," he continued. "Well done again, but it's not over yet, did they tell you about the bikes?" He had to engage them very rapidly.

"No, what bikes?" It was Julie who spoke up first, quickly echoed by Jake: "Do you mean we've got another prize?"

"Yes, I certainly do, come and see." He turned and walked away from them, hoping he had said enough to hook them. They followed him outside eager to see what was in store for them. He clicked the car key and opened the rear door.

"They are just down the road, I'll run you there and back in a moment. Don't worry, it's all arranged." There was a slight hesitation, Julie looked at Jake and seemed to be about to say something, but he jumped in and she followed his lead. He shut the door and went round to the driver's side, got in and started the engine. The Father Christmas suit had apparently worked in instilling confidence.

"Seat belts on kids. Important, don't forget." He heard the belts click one after the other as he released the brake and set the car in motion. From his first words to them inside the library the whole thing had taken maybe a minute and a half. He glanced in the rear view mirror, there were no anxious people at the door of the library, no car on his tail, nothing out of the ordinary to suggest that the kids had been missed yet. By the time that could happen he would be way out of sight.

"My bike's too small for me, I really need a new one," said Julie from the seat behind him. He launched into a conversation designed to fill in the time before they reached the house and stop them thinking of anything other than the bikes. He needed them focussed on that and not to be thinking about what was happening. He asked questions about the competition and their stories and succeeded in prompting them to do most of the talking. Soon the library was left completely out of sight and far behind them.

"Well, I bet you're glad you entered that competition, sit tight the bikes are only a few minutes away and I think the sizes will be just right for you. This extra present is probably because it's Christmas, are you looking forward to Christmas Day?" The kids again responded enthusiastically and they chattered to and fro until, before long, he was pulling into the drive. The Santa suit had proved a complete success in distracting them. The garage was situated at the rear of the house and he drove round and stopped just in front of it completely out of sight of the road.

"Come on you two, chop chop." The children got out of the car and he opened the back door to the house and ushered them inside, leading the way through the kitchen and into the small hall. He was conscious that the kitchen looked oddly unlived in, though there was an old electric kettle and a toaster on one of the work tops. The only other kitchen item was an old mug which he had put in one of the cupboards. This was not something that the children noticed as odd as they hurried after him. He paused briefly hearing them catching up to him then, before there could be any questions, he hurried up the stairs.

"Come along, this way, now what do you think of *that*?" The children were close behind him and, as he stepped aside and pushed the bedroom door fully open so they could see the new bikes propped up standing side by side, new and gleaming, they moved forward into the room to get a proper look.

"Wow, that's cool." said Jake and Julie laughed out loud and spoke almost at the same time. "Looks like that's my size. Can I sit on it?"

There was no answer and when they turned round a second later they found the door was closed and would not open when Jake turned the handle. He was already half way down the stairs when the knocking and shouting started. This was always going to be one of the most difficult bits of his plan, he found it quite upsetting but he went into the kitchen and shut the door, made a mug of tea and waited for the sounds from upstairs to die away. He thought of the rewards to come and that if everything went to plan then it would all be over quite soon.

CHAPTER ELEVEN
Justified, totally justified.

They are just kids, surely they will have just wandered off somewhere, somewhere not far. Margaret tries to pacify Elizabeth Kent who is threatening to go into panic-mother mode.

"Don't worry, I'm sure they must be here somewhere. You stay put and I'll have a look round." She leaves her protesting: "They wouldn't do that." I struggle to be reassuring, then in just two or three minutes Margaret is back, but without the children.

"There's no sign of them, I'll get Philip. He has to know about this." She hurries off to the back premises leaving me to explain to Elizabeth that Philip is Philip Marchington, the library manager. Philip duly joins us after just a few moments. Margaret has clearly described the situation to him.

"Okay, let's see if we can sort this out, shall we? First up, do the kids have a mobile phone?"

"No, well Jake does, but we ration his time on it and right now I'm afraid it's at home." Elizabeth obviously wishes it was otherwise.

"Right, well I have put someone at the door so that we'll see them if they come in or out and all the staff are making a systematic search as we speak. We have a set procedure for this sort of thing. I am sure there is nothing to worry about; maybe they are only hiding. Bear with us a moment, Alice will stay with you, okay?" He glances at me, but hurries straight off, not waiting for my agreement to be a chaperone. I escort the now increasingly distraught mother to a chair in the seating area and again make what I hope are reassuring noises while we wait. Five or six minutes later Philip is back.

"There's no sign of them. I have called the police, again that's standard procedure, and a couple of my team are looking round outside, though I am sure there is no cause for alarm." His face says otherwise. The library is not so big and it appears clear that they are not anywhere in it. I am concerned too, and I only just met them: they seemed to be good kids, sensible and not the sort to wander off. Suddenly Elizabeth's mobile phone rings, she scrabbles about a bit then succeeds in pulling it from her packed handbag, she glances at the screen, her face registering mild surprise and then answers quickly.

"James, you never phone from the office, I... what do you mean shut up and listen?" For a second or two she looks annoyed, but she listens, a look of mounting horror growing on her face and her free hand balling into a tight fist. She punctuates what is being said by only a few words: "What?"... "...at the library..." "...no we can't find them..." "... we just don't know..." finally ending with: "The police are on their way, I'll call you back."

She drops the phone as she lowers her arm and it clatters across the table making a rattling sound.

"I think maybe someone's taken them... my husband... James, has had a threatening note delivered to his London office." She mutters something else under her breath which I think is a swear word. Justified, totally justified. I wonder if it was the letter I saw, it was a little way down the pile, maybe he had not read that at that time.

For a few seconds I can't think of anything to say, I just look at her in horror, then it's too late as Philip returns bringing a police officer to the table.

"This is Sergeant Jane," he says, "I've told her the problem – the kids seem to be lost." The word lost produces an expression on both my face and that of Elizabeth that has him quickly adding:

"Has something else happened?" Elizabeth's face is now lifeless and blank. I speak up.

"It seems possible they've been taken, her husband's just phoned to say that he's had a threatening note of some sort sent to his London office." I add what I think is useful explanation, something that may add credibility.

"He works for Demonaxx, you know the pharmaceutical company that's getting protests about the availability of a new cancer drug."

Sergeant Jane, who I happen to know is Philip's wife – it's a small town, we've crossed paths before and I rate her highly – nods to me and sits down next to Elizabeth. She puts a hand on hers saying: "Let's get things straight." Her tone of voice and the formality of her uniformed figure acts to calm Elizabeth a little as the Sergeant waves the rest of us away. We watch from over at the main desk and can see her talking calmly to Elizabeth, who despite this looks increasingly distraught. The dictionary defines distraught as "very worried and upset". Not enough, not nearly enough; I make a mental note to think of a better word. After a couple of minutes the Sergeant makes a phone call and a few minutes after that a police car draws up outside and several of her colleagues enter the room. A plain clothes Inspector, who I assume is CID, takes charge and a number of us are taken to one side and told we are required to make a statement. Everyone is happy to do so, though I make a call to Becky first to say I have been held up and then manage to get myself high in the order of interviews so that I can get away. Like everyone else there is very little I can say, one minute the children were there, the next they were nowhere to be seen. If they were taken it must have happened in a moment as the event broke up, people were milling about all over the place before the numbers dropped as people left the library. It seems that someone in the police has been in touch with James Kent in London and we hear that he is on his way back to Maldon. We are all asked to list people we saw present;

in my case I knew no one else. Margaret was able to give them details of the teachers in charge of the school party. I suspect all this means that the premise of kidnapping is being accepted. All that over I head off too.

Once I am back in the office it is well into the afternoon. I brief Smaug, telling him we have a real news story on our doorstep, he, needless to say, puts John on the case straight away. I protest a little bit, saying that the children's father is the James Kent who I visited in London about the cancer drug business and suggesting that there has to be a connection. However, it does no good and no involvement comes my way: Yes boss, no boss, three bags full boss. I brief John as instructed, tell him to let me know if I can help – fat chance - and return to my cubicle to find something else to write about, after all those pages won't fill themselves.

My nice manageable little news item about a prize giving in the library has turned into a major crime story but, of course, it's not mine any more. However, maybe if I can keep even a slight involvement in it, I will be able to learn something from it all. Maybe the actual prize giving still rates some coverage and John can't do that; he wasn't there. Lost – kidnapped – children are going to make the next lost dog seem even less interesting than usual.

But wait a minute - I have an idea. I phone Margaret at the library, we talk about it all for a few minutes: weird, scary, terrible for the family, those poor children. And I end by making her promise to phone me if she hears anything that might interest us, something she thinks might add to the story. We are both at a formative stage of our respective careers and I think she understands my hope to get something of this situation working for me. I give her my mobile phone number and she says she will call if anything comes up. And I think she means it, maybe she'll come across something that will help me; I would love to don an investigative hat and discover something that John doesn't. I promise to keep her posted from my end, as the children appear to have been snatched from the library it is only fair to keep the staff there posted.

CHAPTER TWELVE
Another crank

As his children were arriving at the library for their special event, in James Kent's London office he sat staring out of the huge floor to ceiling window that covered most of one wall. It was a spectacular view looking down and across the River Thames far below, a number of boats were moving across the apparently still water under a sober grey sky, but familiarity and his current dark mood meant he hardly saw it. To say it had been a busy period of late was a serious understatement. Very serious. The economy, the market, international competition, the loss of a key member of the Board, all made problems. As ever results were paramount and stakeholders were ever impatient for results. On top of this the press made daily problems with regard to the cost of the company's new cancer drug and so too did a growing number of the public, from those quoting a specific reason to be aggrieved or pleading their individual case to downright cranks taking any excuse to have a go at big business. Now it seemed there were threats to deal with as well. He gave them no great credence but their very existence did not improve his mood. All in all he was having a difficult time.

He had been late getting home every evening for the best part of a month and his wife Elizabeth had moved from her more usual understanding of the pressures of his job to being seriously upset with him. She took on the brunt of the job of caring for their two children, and currently both were at home as Christmas was getting near. A knock on his door returned him to the present moment.

"Your nine o'clock's here." It was his P.A. crisp, efficient and reminding him of his schedule and the visitor he was expecting; who was a senior executive from a major cancer charity. A few moments later she showed her in. She had clearly offered his visitor a drink and put a tray of tea and biscuits down on the desk together with a small pile of post. His public relations people had suggested that were he to refuse to see a representative from this charity it would not look good and was very likely to get another negative mention in the press. Potentially yet more bad publicity that the company could not afford. Usually this sort of thing was not a big story, or it lasted only a short time, but what he regarded as "those idiots at Cure vs Cost" had really succeeded in stirring things up. They seemed to add a new slant day by day and the press continued to run with it, the combination of the emotion of people sick with cancer and the selfish, unfeeling power of big business was proving to be an irresistible combination.

"Good morning, Mr Kent, it's good of you to see me." She was a perfectly reasonable woman representing a well-regarded charity. However, he could have described the meeting as well before it started as he would be able to do after it had finished. She started by praising the drug, the research work and the testing that had seen it emerge and be proved useful and she went on to make a case for it being more reasonably priced so that it could be more widely available. He took a sip of his coffee and tried to appear interested, but he had heard it all before.

Repeatedly. He went through what had become a standard spiel speaking on automatic pilot.

He had resolved to end on a positive note, if she went away with some hope maybe any statement she made later would not be wholly bad.

"As I've said there are two sides to this, we all want the best for cancer patients and the NHS wants to use its resources as best it can, of course they do, no one says otherwise. But companies like ours have to make a profit otherwise research would stop and there would never be another new drug. May I speak to you in confidence?" He looked her directly in the eye.

"I suppose so, yes."

"Right, let me tell you this: the present price won't be the final one. You run a large organisation yourself, you must understand how negotiation works. The opening stance is always high. Think of it this way: if a young child wants a new pet, a rabbit or a guinea pig, say, then the bright one will start by asking for a pony. I am sure we will come to an agreement with the NHS that makes sense to both of us, one that gets this drug being much more widely prescribed. You are right about the urgency, this does need to be sorted, but right at this moment it is all at a rather sensitive stage, there are processes to be gone through, and the least said publically the better. I hope you understand." He said nothing about the long lead time such things normally took or the pressures to maximise profit that was his main intention. Yes, the price would come down and wider distribution would follow, but his job was to make sure the price drop was as little as possible.

"Well, I suppose so, will you keep in touch?"

"Of course, thank you for coming to see me. I know what good work your charity does." She stood up, as did he, they shook hands and she went towards the door. He said goodbye, stifling a sigh of relief that the meeting was over.

"I will try to be patient, Mr Kent, but we want that price down, right down so that every last person who might benefit from this can do so, every day that goes by will see someone who could benefit from it failing to do so," she said as she left. A little later his secretary returned and picked up the tray.

"Your next appointment's at eleven thirty. Anything else for me at the moment?" He grunted and shook his head without looking up and she left, closing the door quietly behind her. Kent picked up the pile of post and papers she had put on his desk earlier. Thumbing through the pile he saw that it was all routine stuff, most important messages came by email of course, but amongst the papers was one unopened envelope. On the front it had the word "Personal" across the top left hand side in bold capital letters. He muttered "another crank" under his breath just as his phone rang. He dropped the letter and took the call. The conversation with someone at the company's Singapore office took a while, there were things to be finalised before the working day finished over there where they were several hours ahead of the U.K. time. After that he checked his email again for the third time that morning and found an important one that needed an immediate answer. The time slipped past in what was proving to be another hectic day.

Finally he glanced sideways across his large desk and saw again the unopened letter on top of the recently delivered pile of post. He lifted a silver letter opener from the desk, slit open the envelope and pulled out a single sheet of paper, his mind still said crank and he was all set to consign it to the waste paper basket, especially when he saw a plain sheet of paper printed with large size type. Then the first sentence brought him up short and focussed his attention as if he had been stabbed by an icicle.

By the time you receive this I will have your children.

He paused for a second, now somewhat rattled, then read on, hardly able to take in what he saw:

**no harm will come to them if… but a payment must
be made and it must be made quickly…
instructions must be followed to the letter… no
second chances… no police…**

The writer asked for £100,000 in used notes packed into
small bundles and gave instructions about delivering it. A
handover had to be made during the morning on the following
day. The last line said:

**Maybe this will make you think differently about
Demoniximol. So many need it <u>now</u>.**

His first thought was: is this true? Surely it was just a
hoax, another damn crank. But it seemed to match the style and
appearance of an earlier note saying that he would be made to
pay. Nevertheless he hoped that its being a hoax was not a vain
hope and realised he had to check further. He remembered too
that Jake and Julie were out at the local library this morning, the
prize giving his wife had scolded him for not attending; he
realised that such a public location might present an opportunity
for abduction. The thought horrified him further and he fumbled
as he got his mobile phone from his jacket pocket and dropped
it on the desk. He thought of his wife, she had been pleased as
punch at the children having won the story competition and
would be revelling in the library event. Then his thoughts were
interrupted as he suddenly became conscious of his secretary
standing at the door, he had not heard her come in.

"It's eleven twenty five – next appointment in a moment."
She was well used to his wanting brevity and spoke in clipped
tones with just enough information to make clear what he needed
to know. He was always so very organised and always well
prepared and ready for visitors and meetings, but this time he
did not ask for her to bring in his eleven thirty. She was not used
to the harsh tone he then used.

"Sorry. No. Hold it a moment. I have to make a personal
phone call."

"But this is…" She never finished the sentence as he interrupted in a loud voice with a brief phrase.

"No! Give me a minute." She had worked for him for sufficiently long to know better than to argue with this sort of tone, a delay was evidently necessary, and she retreated out of the office to pacify his waiting visitor who she knew had travelled into town to make the meeting.

Left alone in the office he picked up his personal mobile phone from the desk and pressed to dial his wife's number. Was the threat real? Were the children okay? He was not encouraged by the fact that she picked up so fast. They spoke briefly, his anger and horror mounting and a few moments later he was telling his P.A. that he was leaving for the day. As her face expressed amazement he knew he had to say something to explain what was highly untypical behaviour. He settled for "family crisis" knowing to his shame that she would still think that weird.

CHAPTER THIRTEEN

Can you do me a favour?

At the end of the afternoon, I leave the office and walk along the High Street, dwelling on the events of the day and beginning to think about what I can eat later this evening. Lacking full concentration as I think I nearly walk straight into someone: it's Margaret. I take a step back and apologise.

"Oops, sorry, I was miles away... but that was quite a day wasn't it?"

"Hi Alice. You could say so, yes, though we are starting to get back to normal in the Library. It's all been a bit hectic and the police took a while to go. Look, I wonder, do you fancy an end of the day drink?" You know what, that would nice and she's right, it has been a hectic day. Unusual too, to say the least.

"Yes, okay, why not? Where shall we go? I think you are more of a local than I am, you should choose."

"If you've got the time, we could walk down to the quay and go to The Jolly Sailor, how does that sound?" I say that sounds fine to me and we walk down the High Street together towards the river both doubtless wondering about the children and speculating about their situation.

"It's dreadful to think about, isn't it, those poor kids, and you can't but help think the worst can you?" My comment only acts to shut us up, we both remain silent for a while, thinking, and my imagined version of what might be happening runs all the way from dark, damp dungeons to torture and murder. I hope I'm wrong. We arrive at the bottom of the hill down by the quay, it's dark but a couple of Maldon's Thames sailing barges are moored alongside each other by the quay and their masts stand out against the clear evening sky. Margaret leads the way into the pub, a blast of warm air rushing out to greet us as she opens the door. I have been here before, in fact Bob brought me here for a drink at the end of my first day, he's not all bad, but I've only been in the better weather when you can sit outside watching the river. Today we repair to an inside corner to sit, both with a glass of lager in front of us. Now we can talk properly and I can't help putting my reporter hat on; I find these days that my asking questions has become a kind of default position.

"Do you know if the police found out anything at the library that might help find out what happened?"

"No, I don't think so, nothing's been said anyway. I know Philip feels bad, he feels maybe there was something we could have done, you know something different in the arrangements for the prize giving that might have prevented what happened."

"Surely it was no one's fault, after all you have kids in the library every day, I'm sure, and no one expects you to guard them, especially from the unlikely event of criminals abducting them. Besides they were with their mother."

"I think you're right, and actually no one is allocating blame, it was just the way Philip felt. Me too to some extent."

"Well, I'm quite sure that neither of you have anything to feel bad about and besides, before it all turned nasty, the prize giving was all going very well. The competition was a great idea – just the sort of thing a library should do. Seems like you have a good boss in Philip, dishing out projects and letting people get on with it. He really had made it your event. At the paper my editor is quite the reverse. I was actually there in the room when the kids were taken, a first-hand eye witness for goodness sake, yet he's given the job of following up what's a major story to someone else, someone more senior. I sometimes wonder if I will ever get beyond having a glorified dogsbody role."

"How long have you worked for the *Express*?"

"Must be about six months now. I always wanted to be in journalism, to write, but it's taking some time to get recognised as someone with anything to contribute other than routine stuff. Between you and me I think of him as Smaug, you know, the dragon from *The Hobbit*". Margaret smiles at this as I add: "I wouldn't say that to his face though!"

"No, I'm sure not. I am sure your time will come though, anyway it must be an interesting place to work."

"I guess so, yes it is, and I do get to check on and write about a good deal, it's just that much of it is of no great consequence; though I must say I've become the world's greatest expert on big birthday celebrations and the most suitable costume to wear for a fun run."

"Surely even routine stuff is important to those involved."

"I guess so. How about you, have you always worked at the library?"

"Since uni I have, yes, home was just the other side of Chelmsford, Writtle, and I originally applied for and missed out on a job at the Chelmsford library. I actually think this has worked out better, though, I get to do a bit of everything and, as you say, Philip is a good boss." We chat of this and that, Margaret is easy to talk to, and I tell her about Jerry, the boyfriend I had at university.

"When we'd done our finals, we went back to different parts of the country, he got a job up north, Leeds, and gradually our contact just tailed away, we went from firm intentions to make it work to growing indifference in a couple of months. I still get an occasional text from him, though I am pretty sure he has someone else in his life now. However, it can't have been a forever thing or I would pine for him, and I don't, not now." We finish our drinks and I say I must make a move and get something to eat; I never seem to have time for anything much at lunchtime.

"We could get a takeaway and take it to my flat, how about that?" Margaret explains she lives in a small flat, the top half of a terraced house at this end of the town. That sounds like a good idea too and we walk back up the hill away from the quay and collect a selection of Chinese dishes from a restaurant at the bottom end of the High Street.

"Come on, it's just down here." Margaret leads the way down a side street, stopping in front of a terraced house and asking me to hold both the food bags while she gets out her key. We enter a small lobby and head up a flight of stairs to another door needing another key. Soon we are sitting in a small living room with the food spread out on a table and a glass of wine each, Margaret having found most of a bottle in the fridge and declaring it to "need finishing". The food is good and the day seems to be ending well, though dark thoughts about the children continue to jump unbidden into my mind. Enough for the moment.

"This is a very nice place, have you lived here long?"

"Yes, well, since I have worked at the library so it's not much more than a year. Any kind of accommodation's difficult isn't it? The cost, I mean. And once I started work I wanted my own place. I don't think I will ever be able to afford to buy a house, even renting can be a problem. My parents helped with the deposit here to get me started. It's good, small but nice I think, and it's convenient to be able to walk to work, and have no commuting costs. But actually I have a bit of a problem at present, in fact I should really put an ad in that paper of yours. I missed the deadline for it last week."

"How's that?"

"Well, I can't really afford this on my own – actually not 'can't really' – I just can't. I had a flatmate, a lodger, a girl who worked in the Maldon Council Offices, but she's moved out and gone to a new job, somewhere, in Braintree I think, I forget the details. I need to find someone else; ASAP before the bills start mounting up." I wonder. I think of the long overdue move I have planned from my dreary tiny bedsit. This may be an opportunity.

"I can put an ad in the paper for you, I could even perhaps get you a discount, but I wonder if I can save you that cost, I'm looking for something like this myself." I waffle on delaying what I feel could be a negative reaction.

"When I got the job I had gone home from uni and was living south of London with my parents. I needed to move to Maldon and I had less than a week between my interview and the starting date. I had to find somewhere to live very quickly, where I am is barely a bedsit, just one room, a bathroom the size of a matchbox and a cooking area on the landing at the top of the stairs. To say it is less than ideal is an understatement, I've been meaning to find somewhere better – and, you know, nicer – for ages but I never seem to get round to it." I stop, wondering if this has given Margaret time to come to a positive conclusion. She gives me broad grin.

"That would be great, I've not relished the thought of finding and living with someone I don't know. When can you move in?" I'm not sure, but I do know it need not be too far ahead. This sounds like a result.

"I'll need to check out the letter about it, but I don't think I have to give more than a week or two's notice, it's a somewhat informal arrangement and was never intended to be permanent."

"Check then and let me know, okay? Maybe a viewing is called for, let me show you round, you've seen this bit, the kitchen's small, but well equipped, it's sort of in an alcove off the living room, see, but both the bedrooms are a good size." She jumps up and leads the way into a good sized double bedroom: bed, wardrobe, chair, small table, bedside cabinets – it's neat, tidy, obviously presently unoccupied and pretty much ready to move into. The bathroom, which she also shows me, has a bath and a shower and is a decent size: something the two of us could share without getting too tangled up, I think. A thought strikes me.

"Hang on, I'm getting carried away, I really need to know about the finances." She runs through some figures: the rent, utilities and so on; I can see it will work. I don't know why I have put off moving for so long, but now suddenly this seems ideal and I'm glad I did nothing earlier. A day of extremes seems to be ending well.

"Yes, sounds as if it should be possible, I'll check about leaving where I am and give you a ring. As long as you're sure." She's professes to be very sure and we prepare to part with an agreement all but made. At last, by happy chance it seems that something I have not been doing anything about for weeks is sorted.

"Well, that's really great, I can't wait to finalise matters. Oh, changing the subject, I wonder if I can ask – can you do me a favour? Will you be going to the Police station in the next day or two?" I am not sure; John's got the job of following up the crime story, but frankly any excuse might be good – maybe I can find out something if I do go in. Sergeant Jane seems inclined to maintain good relations with the local paper and, if nothing else, I want to cultivate that for the future. So, yes, why not.

"Almost certainly will, yes, but why?" Margaret picks up a bag, more of a satchel really, one I remember she carried to the pub and back, and holds it out.

"This belongs to Jake, it was left in the library and it's probably best if it goes back via the police, could you hand it over for me?" Yes, I could; doing them a favour might make me getting one in return just a tiny bit more likely.

"Sure, will do. And thanks so much, flatmate, I'll call you tomorrow." I walk back up the High Street with a spring in my step, though thoughts of the children's plight continue to intrude intent on diluting my good mood. Back in my soon-to-be-left room I am tired, have had a little to drink and just want a quick shower and to fall into bed. As I hang up my anorak, Jake's bag falls on the floor, so does my scarf. I glance at them for a moment, decide to leave them till the morning, and head for the bathroom. I am going to have to learn not to be so messy if I'm to share a flat.

CHAPTER FOURTEEN
Someone's coming

"I didn't think a kidnapper would be like that" she whispered, her lip trembling a little, and her voice sounding loud in the quiet room. "He seemed nice. But he's not, he's really *not*." Julie's voice became even louder and shrill at the end. Then she paused for a moment, and added: "What will happen now? I want to go home." They had lost count of the number of times that they had tried the door, and each time it remained as firmly locked as when they had done so for the first time.

During the first couple of hours locked in the room they had been terrified, distraught, and hardly able to understand or believe what had happened to them. They had clung together and sobbed. They had shouted until they were hoarse, their voices seemingly unheard in what they came to believe was a still, silent, and empty house. And they had tried the door again and again, which lacked any magical change and remained firmly locked. After a little while they noticed a note pinned to the fridge door with a magnet. It was a typed message and only said:

I mean you no harm and aim for this to be finished as fast as possible so that you can go home. There are snacks on the fridge and I will bring you a meal for lunch and then supper later. There should be enough things in the room to keep you busy. Try to be patient.

Over the next hour or so the children calmed down somewhat. They were both still frightened, of course, but with no immediate threat being obvious they finally decided that continuing to shout was getting them nowhere.

All children are curious, even more so perhaps when faced with something unusual, strange or scary. Currently, despite their fears, there was a good deal for them to be curious about and that feeling began to predominate as they began to feel that they could not just sit there doing nothing but fret. So, having sat side by side silently for a little while, Jake, the eldest of them by a couple of years, broke the silence.

"Come on," he told his sister as she again wiped tears from her eyes, "we need to have a proper look and see what's here". Now the initial panic, the shouting and banging on the door that had accompanied their first moments alone in the room, had gradually subsided, more because it could not be kept up for ever than for any other reason, he had decided that they must do something.

In part it was just an instinct. Check things out, he thought, see what's what, and then maybe they could figure out what to do next. It was like writing an essay at school: Jake had recently been told not just to pitch in, but rather to think about it a bit first. How long a piece was he to write, what was the topic, what could be said about it and what would come first, second and so on? He found that doing that worked too. Given an essay or story to write he now always started by making a little plan and it did seem to make the whole process easier. He was old enough to know that things sometimes needed thinking through, so now, he thought, was a time to do just that. It might also stop Julie from crying if she was kept busy, but she was already responding to his idea and wiped her sleeve across her face to dry her eyes.

"Obviously the lights work," Julie said, and her words had both of them glancing automatically up at the two ceiling lights above them without which the room would have been gloomy, "let's see if the television does too".

She went over to the corner of the room, picked up the remote and pointed it at the set, which was small and clearly not very new, but it sprang into life as she pressed the power button and began showing a BBC programme they did not recognise. Julie flicked the remote and the channels changed, she muted the sound and added "That seems fine." The glow of a television picture seemed to inject a small element of normality into the room, but their situation remained unchanged and was not in any way normal.

"Yeah, but what help's that?" Jake asked, and taking the remote from her he switched the set off again and turned away, but he received no reply to his question.

They had never been to the house before and also had no idea where they were. They did a circuit of the small area, which was furnished as a bedroom. Bunk beds set against the wall were neatly made up, an old wooden wardrobe, which Julie inspected next, was empty apart from some elderly wooden coat hangers. There were two comfortable chairs, a chest of drawers, also empty, a small table and a set of large shelves. The room had an en suite bathroom, old fashioned but clean and tidy with soap, shampoo, toothpaste and towels.

"These are new," said Jake pointing to two tooth brushes standing in a glass and wrapped in cellophane packets. The bathroom had no window and a fan high up on one wall started running when the light was switched on.

"There's no clothes, but all sorts of other stuff," Julie said, as she ran her hand along the shelves of the large bookcase.

"It's weird, I wonder whose room it is." They took in the contents of the shelves, noting a box of Lego, and a small selection of books – all second hand paperbacks - that seemed right for their age group and that mirrored the kinds of things they had at home: the Harry Potter books, the three Jasper Fforde books starting with *The Last Dragonslayer* and more. There were also a number of Dorling Kindersley books of non-fiction, a joke book and a variety of notebooks, pencils, paper, paints and brushes. There were a couple of games too: a Monopoly set and a pack of Uno cards, both of these were packed neatly in their boxes.

Julie went next to the window. They had looked at it when they were first in the room but registered only that it was blocked in some way and was allowing only a little light to come in.

"I can't see much," she said, squinting through a small hole. "Just trees, they block the view. It's no help. And this… thingy doesn't help either, what is it? What do we do now?" The view from the window, covered with a metal screen with only small ventilation holes in it, was clearly too restrictive to help them see very much of what was outside or help them identify their location. Julie twisted her fingers in her hair and Jake could see she was again struggling to hold back the tears. He could see no mechanism for opening the screen and realised that it was there to stop them escaping, but he didn't say that.

He looked at his watch, his brand new watch, which told him they had been in the room nearly one and a half hours, and thought back to the events of the morning. Everything had been fine when they had set out for the library. They had had a good time at the prize giving, everyone had been nice to them and Eve Watson had made them feel very special. Getting the new watch had been a high spot for him and he regarded it as very definitely cool. Then the prospect of getting a new bike each had been an exciting extra too. Now, well, just a couple of hours on, things were not fine, they were not fine at all.

"I think we just have to wait," Jake said. "It may not be for long, we just don't know. Do you want something to drink?" He turned to the only other item in the room, the small refrigerator on which they had found the note, and opened the door.

Julie took a look inside. "Coke please," she said at once, seeing the familiar red cans. They were not allowed many fizzy drinks at home, their mother had warned them of the excess sugar they contained, and explained how bad they were for them, but she jumped at the chance of having one now. She opened the can, the sudden fizz sounding loud in the quiet room, and she inserted a straw, taking one from a packet of them visible amongst the things on top of the fridge. Also on top of the fridge there were some crisps, a variety pack of flavours, on a paper plate together with a packet of chocolate chip biscuits that they presumed were the snacks referred to in the typed message.

"There must be something we can do," she said, but Jake could think of nothing and remained silent while he too got himself a drink, opened the multi-pack and put the individual packets of crisps on the table.

"Here, let's eat something, I'm hungry."

They sat together on the lower bunk with their cans and each picked at a packet of crisps, when they took them it seemed like a treat, now they found they were not really so hungry after all. They continued to look round the room. They knew that it had not taken all that long to drive to the house from the library – not much more than three or four minutes - so they must still be local, but that was about it, they had not taken much notice on the drive thinking only of the additional prize they had been told about, eager to see the promised bikes. They did not know the area and neither had any reason to notice the name of the road they stopped in. Jake stood up and went to the door. He knew that doing so was pointless, but he tried it again anyway, it was both depressingly solid and still remained as locked as it was when they had first been left in the room. He looked through the keyhole, there was no key in the lock but the view beyond the room only showed a small glimpse of the banisters outside on the landing. He sat down again.

They were assuredly prisoners.

Julie shuffled closer to her brother and sniffled. Her brother had no answers, but he was sufficiently old to have a feeling that he should be in charge and that he should be the one to think of something, but he was still frightened, they both were. He knew about kidnappings from stories and television but experiencing it personally was, well, it just seemed unreal, though the more he thought about it the worse became the way he imagined that things might end. He knew he must not voice such fears to his sister. The radiator under the window was hot and the room was warm but he gave a shiver.

Then he thought he heard a sound.

He turned his head towards the door beyond which sounds of movement were now faint but clear.

"Someone's coming!" He whispered as the sounds increased and it became clear to them both that there was someone coming up the stairs.

"I thought there was no one there," said Julie, recalling that they had thought they had been left alone in the house, as the sounds increased and now definitely indicated that there was someone approaching the door. They had sat down on the lower bunk again, and now looked briefly at each other and Julie shuffled closer still to her brother before their eyes returned to the door. Their fear heighted, reaching a new pitch, even stifling their urge to shout out.

"Do you think we might get to go home now?" Julie asked, her voice a whisper close to Jake's ear. Then they both looked down to the floor as a rustling sound announced that a sheet of paper was being pushed under the door. The footsteps departed and when nothing else happened, after a few moments Jake got up and went to pick it up.

CHAPTER FIFTEEN
We have to do something

Jake could hear no sound outside of the door as he stooped down and picked up what was clearly a message. It was an A4 sheet of paper with a typed message on it in a largish type size; it was folded in half. He picked it up with exaggerated care almost as if it would explode if treated roughly, using just the tip of his fingers on one corner. He put it down on top of the table.

"Don't touch it Julie" he whispered, conscious that their captor might be listening outside on the landing. "Fingerprints, you know, this could be used as evidence later." Television had clearly left its mark. He used his fingertips to unfold the paper so that they could read the message. It gave him a small crumb of comfort to think of fingerprints and evidence, of a time after this was all over. The message said:

```
I am so sorry. Don't be frightened. I mean you
no harm and will not keep you long. Lunch at one
o'clock. When I knock go into the bathroom and
shut the door, I'll bring the food in and then
knock again so that you know when you can come
                        out.
```

P.S. I hope you like the bikes, you really can keep them.

Unsurprisingly there was no signature. The writer had considered putting *Father Christmas* at the end, but decided against it feeling it was more likely to seem weird and freak the children out rather than to reassure them.

"Looks like a meal is coming quite soon, what do you want to do until then? We have to do something. Okay?" Jake felt it was his job to keep Julie calm, but at the same time he was frightened himself about what might happen, could they believe the part of the note that said they would come to no harm he wondered. He resolved to try to be optimistic.

"We could play Monopoly," said Julie "look there's the box." She pointed to it. Jake remembered the last time they had played at home in a threesome with their mother, the game had gone on forever and had ended, as Monopoly often seemed to, with an argument.

"Not my favourite game, Uno might be better," he countered. "The cards are here and we both like that." They enjoyed playing this game regularly at home, it being a game that is part luck and part skill, is unpredictable and needs some concentration but not so much that whoever is playing it can't chat together too. They got the cards out and it provided a distraction for a while, indeed they found that they got quite caught up in it.

When a knock came at the door a little later Julie was winning by one hand. Jake put this down to the fact that he wasn't fully concentrating, his mind kept drifting away from the game, whereas Julie seemed to have lost herself in it at least for a while and actually she was a pretty good player, though he most often was the winner when they played at home – but only just.

"Come on we better do what he said." They both got up and Jake led the way to the bathroom calling out before he shut the door.

"We're in the bathroom now." He banged the door to reinforce the point.

Jake pressed his ear to the door and, as it was an insubstantial internal one that was hardly necessary, they could both hear a click as the door to the bedroom was unlocked and opened. There were a few other sounds that they could not identify, then the door was closed again and there was a further knocking.

"Okay, that should mean we can come out," said Jake. He opened the bathroom door slowly and peeped out, wondering if it was a trap, he remained frightened and certainly did not entirely believe the kidnapper's odd message saying that he meant them no harm, but the bedroom was empty, the door was closed and a tray had been put down for them. The food had arrived right on time and was evidently from a takeaway: fried chicken pieces, chips and a variety of sauces. It was still hot so could not have come from very far away. There were also a couple of apples and bananas and a medium sized bar of chocolate. It appeared they were not going to be starved to death.

"The food looks alright," said Julie, as she began to help herself, "and there's tomato sauce. It's my favourite." They shared the food out between them, using the plastic plates on the tray, got two more cans of drink from the fridge to wash it down and settled down to eat. Jake paused and put the television on, they only had terrestrial channels, but he flicked through and found them an old animated film to watch. The food was good. When they had finished eating they continued watching the film until its end, each half concentrating and half lost in their own thoughts. It would normally have been something that made them laugh, but today the effect was muted. As it ended Jake used the remote to click off the television.

"Maybe he really does mean us no harm, we have really only heard his voice, the beard and Santa outfit means we have no real idea what he looks like, so we couldn't describe him. If he let us go then it wouldn't mean he was more likely to be caught." Jake was trying to think it through, hoping that such thoughts meant that they would be alright. He wanted to reassure his sister and he wanted to believe in a safe outcome himself too. Then he had another thought, he jumped up and tried the door. It was, as before, locked.

"I thought maybe he had forgotten." He resolved to do the same after every delivery or visit.

Half an hour later, there was another knock and another note under the door.

Please put the tray near the door and go back in the bathroom.

The delivery process was repeated this time for collection. They put the tray down as instructed, holding onto an apple and a banana that they had not yet eaten and called out when they were inside the bathroom. When the exit knock sounded and they came out of the bathroom Jake went straight to the door. Again he found it locked. Whoever it was holding them prisoner did not seem likely to make such an obvious mistake.

"Maybe we could send a note out," said Julie and she went to the window. The metal shutter was covered with a regular pattern of small ventilation holes that were what let in the limited amount of light, it seemed possible that a rolled up sheet of paper could be poked through one of the holes. Jake went over to take a look. The view was limited and he squinted from different angles before coming to a conclusion.

"It would just fall into the garden, no one would ever see it, except if it fell near the back door then the kidnapper would probably notice it. That would be bad, right? Definitely bad."

"What about hanging a sign out?" Jake considered her idea and looked over what had been left for them as he did so. There was a pair of scissors in a pot with various pens, pencils and paint brushes in it.

"You know maybe you could be right," he said. "If we wrote something on a piece of cloth maybe we could somehow get it hanging so that people could see it."

Actually Jake did not know if that was possible, but he reckoned that trying anything was better than nothing and that preparing it would keep Julie occupied for a while. He picked up the scissors and going to the bed he cut a piece, a two foot wide oblong, out of the back of one of the white pillow cases.

"What can we write on it with?" he asked. In response to his question Julie went to the pen pot and returned with a thick black felt tipped marker pen. Jake took it and wrote the single word "Help" in large bold black capital letters across the full width of the cloth. He went over the letters several times to ensure he had a good solid image.

"Now we need some string." They both searched the room high and low but could see nothing. The plan seemed to be still born, leaving escape as far off as ever unless they could come up with a better idea. Neither said anything and Jake put the television on again and they sat quietly together watching it.

The afternoon wore by and at six o'clock on the dot they again heard the footsteps approaching and there was a knock on the door. There was no note this time, evidently the kidnapper expected the procedure to be remembered from last time. They waited a moment, but still nothing came under the door. They went to the bathroom and Jake shouted to indicate where they were as before. They heard the lock click and after a few moments Jake quietly opened the door and peeped out. He was just in time to see the man stepping out of the room. He was again dressed in the Santa suit so there would have been no chance of seeing him properly. As he stepped right out into the room another knock came on the door, the signal that they could come out of the bathroom, followed by the click of the door being locked.

They sat and ate more take away. It was dark outside now and when, a little time after they had finished, and the tray collection procedure had been repeated – with a note left in its place simply saying:

Good night. Breakfast at eight o'clock

Julie got up and went to draw the curtains, an automatic action just as she did in her own room every night at home. Jake watched her doing it and leapt up and joined her at the window. Although the room they were in was furnished and quite comfortable the rest of the house was not, the curtains had been there before the metal screens had been installed, and were obviously old. They were hung only on a thin cord attached to two rings screwed into the wall on either side of the window. As Julie sat down again Jake pointed upwards.

"There's the string we need, we *can* make a sign!" There was a note of excitement in his voice, it seemed to him that this made the plan possible and anyway it made him feel a little better to be doing something, something that might help them get out.

It took a little while, Jake stood on a chair and, by stretching a little, was able to take down the curtains and he then got them the string they needed using the scissors and then unthreading it from where it ran through loops at the top of the curtains. Julie made two holes at the top corners of their improvised sign, receiving a comment from Jake to be careful not to cut herself. Then Jake tied the string to each corner of the cloth and held it up by one point so that the string formed a triangle above the sign. The cloth slumped together a little and prevented the word on it being clearly visible. But when Jake held it up against the wall it flattened out just enough and it looked as if it would work okay. Now they just had to display it.

It took a little while. Again Jake stood on the chair allowing him to reach and poke the cloth through high up so that it would hang flat against the window and hopefully be visible. He opened the window so that he could reach the screen, then started to thread the flag through one of the ventilation holes, he got halfway through then realised the sign was going to face the window instead of having the word showing outwards. He started again and eventually it was done, he made what he hoped was a secure knot to hold it in place and climbed down off the chair. It was dark outside so it would do no good for the moment - but maybe in the morning someone would see it.

When he thought about it realistically he entertained no great hopes. The area behind the house and beyond the small garden appeared to be waste land, they could see no buildings beyond that, just trees, and furthermore they had heard no sound of anyone going past at the back since they had been locked up. Nevertheless Jake had a vision of them escaping, he was sure it must be possible and resolved to go on thinking about it. For the moment he felt better having done something, in fact he decided that was all they could do until morning.

"I don't think we can do any more today, are you tired? Maybe we should get ready for bed." Julie grunted agreement. Jake chose the top bunk and insisted as Julie wanted it too. They said good night, but both found it difficult to get to sleep and they continued to make occasional remarks to each other for an hour or so. Finally Julie fell asleep first and getting no answer to his latest remark Jake soon followed suit. His last waking thought was that he had no great belief that anyone would see their help flag, but it was there and you never knew. Tomorrow would be another day, he had no idea what it would bring, but perhaps they would have new ideas.

CHAPTER SIXTEEN

We are doing everything we can

For all the many problems James Kent had going on at his office, and an early morning look at his emails online had not made that situation appear any better, there was no way he could go to London that day. Not only had some maniac abducted his children on the previous day, but he knew that if he left her side for a single moment his wife would never speak to him again. He had hardly slept, his head was throbbing and he did not look his usual smart urbane self; he had not shaved. He swallowed the last of his second cup of coffee and used it to wash down two Paracetamol. Elizabeth had been given a sedative the previous evening and had, as a result, finally slept better than he had done. She paced the kitchen her breakfast sitting, still hardly touched, on the breakfast bar.

"You should eat something," he said, but she shook her head making jerky movements.

Now they sat in mutual silence at the kitchen table, a police constable was on duty at the door and the Inspector in charge of the case was due to visit in half an hour. James Kent's mind was a mishmash of thoughts both about work, there was so much he should be doing at the office that day, and about the children. He loved his kids, and he well knew that if anything happened to them he would always regret not seeing more of them. His wife thought of nothing but the kids, they were her life. Both his own and his wife's upset was obvious and understandable, few things could be worse than your children being abducted – perhaps only with the exception of the various imagined outcomes which they were both trying not to think about. James Kent's worries reflected what he in fact knew about the situation and that, if anything heightened the dread. His wife's feeling were similarly heightened, in her case from knowing so little.

"How could this happen... and why?" She asked, just out loud as much as to him.

"I don't know," he replied, conscious as he did so that expressing such a view was wholly at odds with the real situation: he knew full well why the family had been targeted.

"How are they do you think? I can't bear to think what their situation might be." Grisly visions began to form in James Kent's mind, but he said nothing. His wife changed tack and continued.

"It has to be linked to your job, that new drug and all the agro that's stirred up." He could see an argument coming and could not think of a single comment that was likely to prevent it. After all he knew it was the truth. He was literally saved by the bell, it seemed that the police Inspector had arrived, he went to the front door to let him in and found him on the doorstep accompanied by a woman police Sergeant in uniform. They had met Elizabeth the previous day, first at the library, then at the police station. He had joined them at the station later but Elizabeth was so upset that the questioning session had been largely curtailed until the morning.

"You have our every sympathy of course and we are doing everything we can. Every lead is being followed and it may help if you answer some more questions for us now. Remember, I'm Sergeant Jane and based in Maldon and Inspector Stuart is with the CID in Chelmsford." Conscious of how they must be feeling, Sergeant Jane began the conversation and made it a gentle start. There had been outrage the previous day that they had insisted on searching the house. It was standard procedure of course, but understandably upsetting nevertheless, somehow especially so when the children's rooms had been examined. Elizabeth had offered them both cups of tea or coffee as they arrived and with that made they sat in a circle in the living room and the Inspector cleared his throat.

Neither of the Kents had ever had any previously had experience of the police. Elizabeth, who loved detective series on television, found the Inspector without any of the quirkiness of his fictional counterparts. Inspector Stuart was unexceptional to the point of blandness and looked like the archetypal "corporate man", dressed in a suit and tie and carrying a briefcase. James Kent hardly noticed his appearance just responded to what proved to be his very professional manner. Elizabeth found his lack of distinctiveness inspired little confidence in his ability to help find the children; her pessimism was reinforced by the fact that there just seemed to be no clues.

"Have you heard any more?" James Kent had given the Inspector the first note he had received, what he had initially seen as just something from a crank. Now the fact that the children had been taken and that the note had contained the phrase; **Action will be taken to make you pay** had been assumed by all to mean that a ransom demand was on the way. Kent knew that this was not in fact the case. Not now.

When Kent had received the full ransom demand and instructions the previous day he had made a rapid decision. Despite that, he felt he had thought it through, after all making decisions was one of the key things he did, it was his job, every day involved analysing situations and deciding on the action he would take in response. It involved making plans too. *No police* the note had said, stressing the necessity for urgency.

He had decided to say nothing about the detailed ransom demand he had received. The time line was short, he thought that if he paid the ransom at once as asked and if then the children were released then the whole wretched business would be over. If their imprisonment did continue despite payment he would have to admit his error and then of course he would have to tell the police more, to own up and be advised as to what should be done next. To his business brain his initial approach made perfect sense, it would provide a quick fix, and a rapid return to normal. The ransom note was safe in his briefcase and would stay there for the moment, out of sight and known only to himself.

He had made all the necessary arrangements before he left the office, the company bank had not asked questions about the money, or rather they had in fact asked a number of questions but he had successfully brushed them aside. He was used to getting what he wanted, besides Demonaxx was a big international client for the bank and no one there was about to risk upsetting the CEO. He had collected the money himself. Right now the money would be with a trusteed aid, the only person he had taken into his confidence, and then only to a very limited degree, no mention of money had been made. Now his plan was set to play itself out. He had convinced himself it would work and that all would then be well.

"No, I've heard nothing more yet." He said firmly glancing at the telephone on the table nearby, "you will record any call that comes won't you?" He knew a call demanding a ransom would not occur given the arrangements he had made, but he wanted to keep the police from knowing what he had done, and of interfering with it, but he also wanted to give the right impression.

"Yes, all that's in hand." Arrangements had been made the day before, a technician had spent time in his study where the house phone line originated rigging up equipment that could both record calls and trace them. Tracing could not be done instantly, it took time, and the Kents had been instructed to keep any caller talking for as long as possible. The Inspector opened his battered leather brief case and took out a fat folder of papers.

"This new drug of yours seems to have been causing some problems, doesn't it, Sir?" He explained that the papers were copies of all the letters and emails complaining or protesting about the drug pricing issue. These had been obtained from Kent's office the day before and sent by special courier to Maldon. At the mention of the drug protests James Kent felt duty bound to launch into a defensive statement.

"It's an important new development, trials have gone well and I don't doubt it will be widely available on the NHS in due course, we are in negotiations and these things take time. Meantime these sorts of angry messages are normal, just par for the course, something that goes with the territory, so to speak. It's usually no more than cranks and people who know nothing about how these things work that send such things and many are anonymous." In some ways the more time it takes the better he thought.

"I understand that, Sir, nevertheless we must explore every possibility, it could be that the kidnapper is amongst these people, and there are quite a few, we are also investigating the many people *complaining* on social media and that makes it a large number of possibilities in all. We are speaking to people at the protest group, you know Cure versus Cost, as well, though their leader denies all knowledge of this." He put special emphasis on the word complaining, clearly implying that many were worse. He continued: "It all takes time, time we do not have, so if any of these people are known to you, especially if you can think of anyone who might have a particular grudge or a motive to do this, maybe there is someone here who's crossed swords with you on other issues, then we need to know about it. We must go down the list." Kent accepted that and said so. For the moment he was grateful to be kept busy.

As the Inspector went through the names, a process punctuated by Kent regularly saying a dozen versions of "Never heard of them", one or two names had come up about which he made a comment.

"He's a shareholder in the company, been a thorn in the side at every shareholders' meeting for years and has always seemed to have a particular dislike for me," he said of one, adding: "But surely someone's not going to write such a letter, a letter including his name and address and then kidnap our children. That makes no sense at all, does it?"

"Maybe not Sir, but we have to be thorough and stranger things have happened."

Every time a name had something to be said about it, the Inspector made a note and passed it to Sergeant Jane who would send a notification of it back to their HQ so that the circumstances could be checked later. It took a while to go down the list, though few of the names drew any comment from James Kent. Elizabeth was asked questions too but she was unable to think of anything that pointed a finger at anyone she knew. She remained convinced it was all linked to James's company and she knew only the basic facts about that, commenting that "He doesn't bring work home."

Finally questions, and the file of papers, seemed to be exhausted and the police began to take their leave, though a police constable remained in case a phone call came in on the landline. Again Sergeant Jane made encouraging noises as they left.

"I know it's hard for either of you not to worry, but you should try to stay calm and let us know at once if you think of anything else, however insignificant it seems, especially if you can think of anyone, anywhere who might have any reason to hurt you. And be assured we are doing everything we can. We will let you know at once if there is any news."

No sooner had the front door shut behind them than Kent's mobile phone rang. He looked at the number, glanced at his watch and answered, walking over to the window and looking out into the garden as he did so; he did not want his wife to overhear this call. Speaking over his shoulder as he went he said simply "Office." It was a word he knew guaranteed that she would ignore what was said.

"Yes, tell me what's happening?"

"The delivery went well, all as planned, but when I tried to follow him he lost me. I don't know where he went."

"You what! You idiot, how could you do..." Kent was interrupted, his aid was keen to avoid taking the blame.

"He had anticipated being followed, he was ready for it and he had a plan. Clever too. I think you are dealing with someone professional." He briefly explained the ruse the man he had attempted to follow had used.

Kent was stunned, he had been so confident in his plan, the payment might still lead to the kids' release, but this, which he regarded as in the nature of insurance, had not worked and could not lead to the kidnapper being found. He ended the call without a further word. The situation now seemed even bleaker and he wondered if what he had done was the right thing, he wondered too if he had misjudged the situation, maybe the children were in even graver danger than he had first thought. But for the moment it seemed all they could do was wait. He turned back to his wife wondering how either of them was going to get through the day.

CHAPTER SEVENTEEN
I may have something

After my evening with Margaret I am up and about in good time, and consider a couple of personal chores that need attention. I eat toast as I make a circuit of my tiny room trying to remember where I put the details about my rental arrangement; I find them in an envelope propped behind a jar on the kitchen worktop. I put them there way back, in plain sight, supposedly as a visible reminder to my need to find a better home, but Potterlike they soon took on a cloak of invisibility. I put the toast down, perch on the arm of a chair and open up the envelope to check. I discover that I only have to give a week's notice. That's great, I make a note to phone Margaret later on and also to ask her about an agreement between the two of us, however informal our arrangement I reckon we should have a note of it in writing. It's what my father calls pear-shaped precautions: that is the thought that friendly arrangements that appear in need of no formality can suffer from a lack of them if a relationship should ever change for the worse. I am sure Margaret and I will get on perfectly well, but I'll still suggest we have a written note.

There is very little stuff in my room both because I have never seen it as a permanent abode and because it is so tiny, when I move on I will need to make a trip back to my parents to collect some more of my stuff. Something that is here is a computer and a printer. I sit for a minute and compose a short note to my landlady saying that I am moving on and thanking her for taking me on at such short notice when I started to work in the town. It might not have been my ideal home, but it gave me a good start and has been convenient. The note can be delivered once I have spoken to Margaret again – in case she has had second thoughts. I put it in my bag, hoping I can stick it through the landlady's door downstairs when I get back at the end of the day. I gather up the bits I need for today's work, including Jake's bag, and head out to go to the office.

*

I am eating a lunchtime sandwich at my desk, a bog standard cheese and tomato one made at home before I came out as I can't afford to buy posh ones in the High Street. I also have a single banana, not enough to make me glow in the dark, but a good source of energy so I'm told. I am taking a brief pause from writing about a local resident who evidently won a pie eating contest; really, who cares? Honestly, some of the things Smaug considers appropriate for our beloved paper are just such a nonsense; this was not even a charity event. I am pleased all is fixed regarding the flat share. I phoned Margaret before I got down to any work earlier on and everything is arranged. I have a new home and a moving date is set. I also sent an email to my mother telling her the news and explaining that I would need to pick stuff up from my old room.

As I eat I can't stop thinking about those poor children. Whatever happened it must have been well planned, in the general hubbub following the prize presentation by all accounts no one noticed a thing; the children were probably gone in a moment. John's out trying – again - to get some information from the police, but personally I don't think it will do any good, they don't know anything much yet, though rumour has it that a ransom must be involved and that seems logical enough to me. I have to say I did not warm to James Kent when we met in his palatial offices, but his wife seemed nice enough and the kids were great. I feel so sorry for the poor woman – and the kids too, of course, it's a real worry.

I take a sip of coffee and consider Jake's bag and when I might take it along to the Police Station. If John comes back with nothing, but I could get something that would be a result. I sip my coffee again and idly I open up the bag. The first thing I see is a library book, a hardback, I can tell it's a library one as it has a transparent plastic cover over the paper one. I once heard this practice described as being not to keep the dirt out, but to keep it in, something that was probably said about a title like "Fifty Shades of Grey". Like anyone who loves books, I think, I am always interested in what other people read, even a child. This one's a mixture of magic and detection, a book by Derek Landy in the Skulduggery Pleasant series. He obviously likes this author's books as this is number three in the series. I can't help being nosey and rummage deeper, there's an envelope which I imagine contains the book voucher from the story prize, a half-eaten bar of chocolate (which I resist finishing), a less than clean handkerchief (which I leave be), a copy of a children's news magazine (which I applaud), a pair of gloves and the box his prize watch came in. I look at the picture on the packaging, the watch case is a bright orange colour, it has a black strap, and the face of it looks as if multifunctional is a highly inadequate way to describe it. It clearly appealed to Jake as he had it out of the box and on his wrist within moments of receiving it. A much folded sheet of white closely printed paper is sticking out of the box: the instructions. He obviously didn't take the time to read those. It looks like a large sheet and only a part of it is in English. I ought to get back to my consideration of pie eating, but I scan the headings, most are the kind of words you would expect, Settings, Display, Sounds, Security - but one pings out at me: Tracking location. This brings me up short: is it possible that the phone signals where the wearer is currently located? In which case....

My phone rings. It's the pie eater.

"Yes, this is Alice Carter. Thanks for phoning back, Malcolm, I just had one question about this pie eating thing you won... Yes, an amazing number, very, I don't know how you did it and I will be sure to mention it, but did it win you a prize?"

"A cup, I got a cup. It's engraved, like." It's also absolutely like... frankly words fail me. A pie eating cup – I pray this is not the highlight of my day, but wish him well and put the phone down. And maybe it won't be, I turn back again to the instructions for Jake's watch. Bloody hell, it looks as if this gadget might actually be able to locate the kidnapped kids. I scan the details and become ever more certain, if I have this right then the watch has a feature that sends some sort of signal to a computer or a mobile phone.

I am not the most tech-savvy person in the world. I use a computer a lot for work, but that's mostly word processing and Googling for information. But I can work a fair amount of stuff, I use Facebook, Twitter, WhatsApp and the like, though I'm not into gaming. More of a words person.

Ten minutes later I am still puzzling over it. I think I'm right, but just because it can send a signal, if it can that is, I am still not daring to be a hundred percent sure, doesn't mean it's busy doing so right now. It may need all sorts of set up processes to be gone through.

Technology is both wonderful and difficult to keep up with these days, much of it originates in the Far East; the leaflet for the watch says it was made in Japan, so no surprise there then. It has instructions in maybe ten different languages, so the number of pages to be read is less than it appears at first sight, and once you concentrate solely on the pages in English it should be straightforward. However, if there is one thing the Japanese are not so good at it is setting out clear instructions in English. Things don't get lost in translation so much as mangled beyond all reasonable likelihood of understanding. If I remember right I have an electronic gadget somewhere the instructions for which say things like, Install with adjust this machine current public affairs to cut the power supply necessarily. Too often instructions are labyrinthine and seemingly more geared to help you make a wild guess than provide a clear route to accurate operation.

I sit with the instruction sheet spread out in front of me, all thoughts of competitive pie eating forgotten, as the minutes tick by. Good grief, why are these things never straightforward? Even this one short section is confusing. Gradually it becomes clearer, it should link to a phone, or a computer, but a phone would better on the move. I get my mobile out and am already imagining finding and freeing the children and the headlines that will follow as I do so. Ridiculous, I should just hand all this over to the police. Needless to say I decide to take it a bit further first, after all, I do not want to present them with something that proves to be rubbish. I reckon I'm closer to working this out now: I'm pretty sure it needs an app.

I go into the Google Store on my phone, type in the name of the app specified and click on Install. Bingo, it's going through the process of loading something. It ticks through percentages to show that it's making progress and yet it takes forever, or it seems to. First, it's downloading, then initiating... finally it's done. Right, or rather right?

The phone on my desk rings again. I consider ignoring it, but, conscious that Smaug would probably be aware of my doing so if I let the ringing run on as he is currently in his lair with a clear view of me at my desk, I pick up.

"Alice, hi, it's Margaret, you know flatmate, librarian and ..." I interrupt her in mid-sentence.

"Yes. Hi, what is it?" That was a bit abrupt, I think we would both count each other as friends now, we had a nice chat yesterday evening and now I have a nice new home to go to. I should be more polite. "Sorry, sorry, I'm just a bit distracted. What can I do for you?"

"I was just wondering if we could meet again this evening, get things finalised about the flat, get something in writing, nothing too complicated, just..." I am doing it again, interrupting, and as I do so I have a thought, I have to involve Margaret in this.

"Sorry, again, I keep interrupting you, and yes we should meet, no problem, but there's something else. It's..." Margaret gives as good as she gets and interrupts me.

"You're not having second thoughts are you, about moving into the flat, I mean?" I try to put real urgency into my voice.

"No, no, please listen, please: I may have something. About the children, you know. Well I think I do. So it's important and I'd value your help. Look, can I pick you up in the car outside the library, it's urgent, can you come now, right now? I'll fill you in when we meet up."

"Well I suppose I could, I was just about to take a break for lunch, but what on Earth is going on and why the urgency?"

"Trust me, I'll explain when I see you, five minutes, look out for a battered old blue Mini, okay?" I can almost feel her brain straining to say something else, doubtless a question, but she resists and all she says is: "Alright, see you in a few minutes."

CHAPTER EIGHTEEN
We may be about to find out

I put the phone down and pick up my coffee mug; it's cold. I'll just go. I stuff my mobile in my bag and wonder if I should take my laptop too. Yes, maybe I should, just in case. I unplug it, checking the battery is okay as I do so. It is, of course it is, the thing's been plugged in as I've worked on my pie eater story, so I slip it into its case and head for the door. Becky's at lunch, so I can't tell her what I'm up to. No matter. Maybe this is my break, maybe this is something that will give me a genuine piece of news, something I'll be really proud to write up and have a by-line on. Smaug doesn't need to know about it at this stage, besides it could still all come to nothing.

I slip into my anorak as I hurry down the High Street, swapping my laptop case from hand to hand as I do so. My car is where I left it in the main town car park, a battered old Mini-Countryman with the old fashioned wooden trim along the back and sides, it would hardly be high on any thief's list of desirable cars. But I need a car for work and, given my wages, this must suffice for the moment. Despite the cold it starts first time.

Margaret is already standing outside the library waiting for me, she is hugging herself against the cold as I draw the car to a halt right next to her. It's really not taken me much more than five minutes to get here since she phoned. She gets into the passenger seat and shuts the door. The car has not had time to warm up yet, it's as cold inside as it is out. No matter.

"Now what's all this about, you made it sound intriguing?" Margaret displays excitement alongside uncertainty, one hand twisting her hair into a tangle behind her ear as she speaks. Just as I'm about to explain myself, without warning there is a banging on my side window which make us both jump. It's a man in dark uniform: a traffic warden. Not good timing.

"You're stopped on a no parking line," he says raising his voice to penetrate the closed window and waving what is probably a book of parking tickets at me as I turn to face him, getting ready for an argument. But Margaret intervenes.

"Drive behind the library we have a private area of parking space for staff there." I ignore the warden, barely biting off the urge to curse at him though I suppose he's just doing his job, I press the button to start the engine and drive on round the corner. Once parked I look at Margaret in what I hope is a suitably apologetic manner.

"Thanks. Okay. Here's the thing. Did you see the prizes the kids got?" I was going to ask them about that at the prize giving, I wanted a reaction from them as well as just the facts, but of course the opportunity disappeared; as did they.

"Book tokens, as I remember, but how is that any…" I interrupt again before she can make her last utterance into a coherent question. I dig in my pocket and hold out the box with a picture of the bright orange watch on it. She looks at it quizzically and waits for me to explain further.

"Not just book tokens, come on – you fixed it all. They each got a watch as well, remember? This is the packaging for the watch Jake got, he loved it, he got it out and strapped it on straight away. Julie got a different one that's… well, I know not where."

"Okay, I remember, but so? Jake can tell the time. How does that help?" Margaret is beginning to sound just a touch impatient and is clearly wondering where all this is going. So I get to the nub of the matter.

"It's electronic – smart - watches can do so much these days, link to other things, tell you that you've just received an email, sound an alarm, make toast...whatever." I pause, maybe for effect, maybe just to take a breath, I don't know, but I realise I have to get to the point. Perhaps I could have gone about all this rather better.

"I looked at the instructions and one of the things this one seems to do is monitor where the wearer is – I think it knows their location. It's has a tracker feature designed specifically to keep children safe. It works through an app, I have discovered that much and had just put it on my phone when you rang. Then I thought, we have to do this together, we may have the answer. But we need to look at the instructions again and work it out properly." Margaret looks suitably stunned and for a moment says nothing, then:

"That's amazing. Well spotted you, I hope you're right, if this shows where the children are then... wow, that's, that's... let's have a look or should we just take it to the police and let them work it out?" I find myself torn between the urgency for action to rescue the children and my fledgling newshound's desire to crack the thing myself. Well, ourselves. I've decided that Margaret has to be involved too after all.

"Five more minutes, okay? Let's see if we can actually make it work and find out exactly what it does." Margaret nods her agreement, I spread out the instructions between us, point to the bit about location and we read over it together.

"Wait a minute, I think it's just the app we need to look at now." That should be much more likely to be solvable, I do all sorts of stuff on my phone. Smaug even gives us an allowance towards a good one as everyone on the paper uses them so much for work, just as well on the wages he pays me.

"So, what do we do then?" Asks Margaret and I hold my phone between us so that we can both see the screen.

"Right, now let's see what it does." I click on the app to open it and the first thing that seems to be necessary is to create a password. I type in the word Margaret. She watches me do it and gives me a funny look.

"Well, they were in your library," I say as my screen immediately tells me that the password is invalid and must include a number. I go through it again using my birthday; idiotic, I know, anyone would find it so easy to break all my codes, though most people are less careful that they should be. The new version of the password is accepted.

"Now we should be able to link up to Jake's watch, but we don't know what the code for that is." What now? Think. Think. I look back at the instruction sheet.

"Wait a minute there's a factory setting. If he's not changed it, and I bet he's not even thought about it, then his may be the only watch that reacts if we send a signal." I double check the instructions. "No, wait a moment, it seems we just put in the serial number of this particular watch. Where's that shown?" A moment's more investigation and I have found and entered it.

"It's possible the kids are too far away now, I suppose." We are not there yet and Margaret's right to be sceptical, but I *so* want this to work.

"I think the signal goes up to a satellite and down again, it's like a sat nav, and it should make contact wherever the watch happens to be." We stare intently as the app chugs through various screens and then a map appears in front of us. It actually only takes a couple of seconds for that to happen, but our eagerness makes it just seem much longer. On the map a red star is flashing, but on the phone's small screen it isn't clear what geographic area the network of small roads shown on the map is depicting.

"Where is..." I interrupt Margaret's half formed question.

"I need to use the zoom, give us a sec." I find the plus and minus signs and a moment later we find ourselves looking at a map of Maldon.

I can hardly believe it, neither of us can. We exchange a glance and I audibly suck in my breath.

"If we are doing this right then the kids are still right here in Maldon – and not that far away either." At this Margaret lets out a whoop, but if she is more excited than me I would be greatly surprised – I still have possible dramatic headlines in mind. I juggle some more with the zoom to find where the star is located. We still don't know exactly where this is leading us, but neither of us suggests going to the police at this stage. There seems to be an unspoken desire to test it out, though neither of us voices anything like a plan, I do specify action.

"Right, you hold the phone while I drive, it's showing somewhere down towards the bypass, beyond the pub opposite Arcacia Avenue."

I drive out of the library yard, skirt the car park, alongside which the traffic warden is writing a ticket next to an empty car, and head for the road leading to the Maldon bypass, a road that so many people ignore that it totally fails to stop the town's ancient narrow High Street from being a traffic nightmare from morning to night. I'm barrelling down the straight stretch to the roundabout and so far the red star is staying steady. I turn left down Arcacia Avenue, and note that the pub on the corner is called "The Queen Victoria"; of course it is.

"Can we really have located them?" Asks Margaret. I don't know enough about this watch gadget to know whether we have or not, and I don't dare assume it's have. But if we do think we've found them, then what do we do next? Will it pinpoint a single house or building or only a general area? And what then - do we just go and knock on doors and ask anyone who answers them whether by any chance they happen to be a kidnapper? Any kids locked up in the back room have you, Sir? Maybe it is time to call the police, though I would *so* love to see the headline "Star reporter rescues kidnapped children". Hold up: we need to get to the end of the trail first.

"We may be about to find out."

There really is a warren of streets back here, Maldon is a larger place than I sometimes think. I have slowed right down, a horn sounds somewhere behind me and a large black BMW overtakes us. The driver throw us an exasperated look as he goes by; impatient bugger, he has no idea what we are doing. I signal and make a right turn, following the signal on the screen, and we drive slowly down a road lined with houses on both sides. The map seems to show we are nearly there. I am jolted out of my thoughts by Margaret speaking up alongside me. She sounds worried.

"Look ahead, we seem to be coming to a dead end." I see we are and slow to a stop and pull up by the kerb. There is a single house ahead of us. I turn off the engine and glance to my left where Margaret is holding out the phone indicating the screen with a finger.

"It seems to indicate dead ahead, so it appears to be flagging up that house," she says, pointing straight ahead through the windscreen, "shall we call the police now?" I still have the scent of a bigger story than that we just led the police here.

"No, not yet, we have to be sure, let's check it out ourselves first. It would be unfortunate to tell them about something that proved useless." By which I really mean let's see if we can rescue them ourselves and give me the news story I so long for.

If this gadgetry has worked as I now think it has and if the children are there that is; and if we don't end up facing someone with a gun and a pronounced wish not to be apprehended for their crime. If, if, if... I resolve to go carefully.

"We can do this," I say and turn off the ignition.

CHAPTER NINETEEN

Maybe, just maybe.

We both get out and I lock up the car and zip up my anorak against the cold. The road, a typical residential street, seems empty with seemingly no one else around. I look back the way we have come and the only movement I see is a car pulling out of a drive more than a hundred metres back and driving away.

We walk forward taking our time, looking around as we go, the house in front of us appears ordinary enough if somewhat run down, the short strip of front garden is a bit overgrown, the windows are dirty and there is a good deal of peeling paint. An estate agent's "Sold" notice is positioned at the gate, lolling at a slight angle. It's all quiet and silent and I reckon it could be the place. Certainly I reckon we need to check it out.

"Let's walk right round and have a look." I have considered just walking up to the front door and knocking but rejected that idea out of hand, at least for the moment. It seems clear that whoever kidnapped the children did so to get at James Kent who is not, after all, the most popular man in the pharmaceutical industry at present or indeed in the country. The police have said nothing about a ransom, but I suppose that might come later. I don't expect it was out and out gangsters that took the children, more likely activists, maybe even someone with a genuine concern for the harm the company's attitude could be doing to some people, but whoever is responsible I still worry in case someone is watching us and I certainly do not want a direct confrontation with them. I hold a finger to my lips to indicate to Margaret that we should be quiet and lead the way up the front path.

The front door is old fashioned, wooden and has long needed a coat of paint. It is also solid with only a small frosted window set high up, making sure there is no way to see inside. I continue round the left hand side of the house where there is a small window that proves to allow us to look onto the hall inside. It's dirty so I give it a rub and look through: I see only a small, blurred glimpse of stairs and banisters. The bannisters have a bright red coat or cape of some sort hanging over them at the bottom. No real help there. Then a thought strikes me. I move on a little and turn and whisper to Margaret.

"I think we might be in the right place, what looks like a Father Christmas suit is hanging over the banisters. Makes sense, I seem to remember that there was someone at the prize giving wearing one and it could have provided them with a way of luring the children away."

"And acted as a disguise as well," says Margaret. She makes a fair point, I agree.

After a moment we move along a side path to the back corner of the house, on the way looking through another window that shows us a grimy image of what looks to be a sparsely furnished living room. At the far end the path is blocked by a fence stretching diagonally from the garage at the back of the house to the wall. It's somewhat rickety but it has barbed wire on the top and there's no gate so we will need to retrace our steps to get round to the back. We look up and the angle allows us to see just a little of the back of the house. As far as we can see all the upstairs windows appear to have curtains across them. Then I notice something fluttering in the light breeze. There is a flag of some sort hanging against one of the upstairs windows. I crane my neck to see round the corner and can just make out that it has the word "**Help**" written on it. Bold and black. There is still nothing to be heard around us and I turn and signal Margaret to go back to the front and, as we retrace our steps, I tell her about the flag.

"There's a flag hanging out of one of the windows at the back, it says "Help", we must definitely be in the right place and those kids are not just sitting there if they managed to put that out. Let's go right round to the back. Maybe there's a door there and we can get into the house."

I move on still half turned towards Margaret over my shoulder and trip over a tangle of wire. I don't fall over but stagger a little. We stepped over it without any problem going in the other direction but this time I have obviously not taken sufficient care. The plastic covered wire is attached to a steel post leaning against the wall that probably once acted as a clothes line. My inadvertent tug on the wire pulls the post away from the wall, it totters for a moment and then falls headlong into what we have identified as the living room window. The crash and sound of breaking glass seems to shatter the comparative silence around us and seems also to linger in the air for a long moment. I swear under my breath and hear Margaret do the same, my words are the worst, but then I would expect no less, she's a respectable librarian. We freeze and stay virtually motionless for what seems like an age. Nothing. We hear no sound and no one comes running out to investigate. It appears that if the kids are there they are there alone at present.

The top half of the window is smashed, only a ragged ring of glass is left around the frame. I immediately see it as an entrance; it's a way in. I have absolutely no democratic thoughts in my mind of any sort at that precise moment, only a further vision of possible headlines, and a rapidly formed conviction: someone must go in and that someone must be me.

"We can't *not* take advantage of this Margaret, there's now a way in, I'll climb in and explore, you stay here and shout if anyone comes, yes – at once and loudly please." Margaret hesitates before speaking looking somewhat uncertain.

"You don't think it would be better to call the police now do you?" No, I really, really don't. We may be wrong or we may rescue the children, but we have to try; I see those headlines again.

"A quick look first, okay. I'll be careful and I'll be out before you know it, please, you stand guard." I do not wait for her approval, I lift the pole out of the window and lay it on the ground, being careful not to make any more noise, I then reach over the broken glass with some care and undo the window latch so that I can slide the bottom half up. It's stiff but I manage to do this and then put a leg over the sill and into the room. My foot can't avoid the broken glass inside and makes a crunching noise that I imagine echoing around the house. I wait a second, grateful that I'm wearing sensible shoes, still hear nothing and then get my other leg through. Inside I stand up and look around. It is a living room, but it does look as if the house has been unoccupied for a while. There is some basic furniture, an old three piece suite, a coffee table and a sideboard, but nothing else: no television, no curtains, no ornaments, nothing except a generous coating of dust. The carpet has seen better days and has a large, dark stain in front of the sofa. I look back at the window.

"Stay put, I promise I'll be quick." Margaret says nothing in reply, which I am taking to mean acceptance. I don't give her a chance to say otherwise and move on away from the window, but having told her I will be quick I now feel compelled to move slowly – and to remain quiet. I cross the room and open the door an inch at a time. I can still hear nothing. The room opens onto the hall and I move to the front door but find it locked in a way that won't open from the inside without a key. The garment slung over the bannisters right in front of me is definitely a Santa outfit, bright red with white trimmings; a fluffy white beard clinches it. Finding the front door locked, and concerned to know there is a way out other than the window, I step along the corridor, being careful to make no noise, to what I can see is a kitchen at the end. I try the back door, this is also locked but has a key in the lock which I turn and open the door. I look out onto the garage and back garden and still hear nothing. I shut the door again and head for the stairs.

Still worried that there might be someone about to spring out on me I go up step by step with care, while also moving a little quicker now. There are several doors leading off the small landing, one, pretty much in front of me as I get to the top, is ajar, I push the door so that it swings wide and see a bedroom furnished with bunk beds, but empty of children. A door inside stands open showing a small bathroom beyond: it's also empty.

I am becoming more confident that I am alone in the house now and move faster, opening the first of the other doors and being startled by a sharp banging sound to my left that makes me almost jump out of by skin. It comes from behind the door, when nothing else happens I move the door a little and peep behind it only to find an old wooden coat hanger has fallen from a hook behind the door. The room is otherwise empty apart from a single bed with no mattress. I go on to find another empty bedroom and a bathroom that any television property programme would regard as ripe for a facelift. I have no inclination to linger long in the house and hurry downstairs, go back into the living room and clamber out of the window to find a relieved Margaret hopping from one foot to the other; she can see that I'm alone.

"Thank God you're alright, what did you find?"

"The place is empty, it looks very much as if the children have been here, I'm sure they were, there's one properly furnished room upstairs, but there's no sign of them now. If they were here then they must have been moved." And that's not good news, I imagine that they could be anywhere in the country by now.

"Let's get out of here, this place is giving me the creeps." Margaret has a good point and I've already been given a fright by a rogue coat hanger.

"Okay, yes we'll go. But let's check the garage at the back first just in case. Come on." I lead on at once in case Margaret should protest.

We retrace our steps round to the front of the house and Margaret tries the front door as we go past. No surprise there, I have already discovered that it's locked, but Margaret suddenly seems to be getting bolder.

"Just the garage and then we'll get out of here." Having found the house empty, my hopes that we may actually find the children have diminished, but a tiny glimmer remains, after all the watch did seem to have led us right here. Maybe, just maybe.

"Okay. It seems right, sort of place you would expect, and then there's the flag and the Father Christmas outfit, you're right, that makes sense too. I suppose we should give the garage a go." Margaret speaks in a stage whisper.

There seems to be tacit agreement to this plan and we both keep walking along the front of the house aiming to go along the drive on its right hand side and round the corner to the garage. I still can't help being conscious that the kidnapper might reappear any minute and I am pretty sure the same thought must have occurred to Margaret. It is probably no accident that the words "ruthless" and "kidnapper" go so naturally together; the dictionary says that ruthless means "having no pity or compassion", not the most comforting thought right now. Whoever's responsible they might well be armed and I don't want a news story to be about Margaret or myself getting shot. Nevertheless, given that all the signs right now are that the kidnapper is elsewhere at present, I make less effort to be quiet this time, I speed up and get a stride or two ahead of Margaret. The garage is round the back, but as I get to the corner of the house something whacks me on the side and sends me flying backwards onto the ground. I'm surprised and shocked rather than hurt, but there's a weight pressing me down; I struggle to get up, but I can't move.

CHAPTER TWENTY

I may have an idea

After their night as prisoners Jake and Julie were awake early the following morning. Jake woke first, looked at his watch and saw it was only just after half past six. He knew, as he took in his unfamiliar and scary surroundings that he would not get to sleep again and as he stirred and got out of bed, climbing down from the top bunk, Julie woke up too. She looked slowly around the room, the horror of their situation evidenced by the unfamiliar surroundings returning to her mind and her sorrowful face said it all: they were still prisoners.

"Mum and Dad must be looking for us, they will won't they?" Said Julie, searching for a crumb of hope, but seeming also to be on the point of dissolving into tears.

"Yes, and the police too," said Jake "let's get dressed and then we'll see what we can do. You go in the bathroom first." After they had taken turns in the bathroom he put on the television and found an early morning children's programme. They sat and watched, neither spoke, each only half concentrating on the programme and yet unsure what to say to the other. If they had put on the local news channel they would have seen no report of their abduction; the police, despite the Kent's protestations, were currently holding fire on any public announcements until after the expected ransom note or message had arrived. Though the window was largely blocked in due course they could see that it was daylight.

"Maybe someone will see our flag now," said Julie, remembering their efforts of the evening before. Jake did not reply as just then there was a knock on the door; it was exactly eight o'clock. Breakfast. No note this time. They looked at each other for a second but went to the bathroom from where Jake shouted out that they were inside. They heard the room door open, then Julie gave a sudden loud scream.

"Let us out. Let us out. Let us out!" She was shouting at the top of her voice. She reached for the bathroom door handle, but Jake held her back.

"No. Don't, if we see him he may hurt us. We have to wait." The bedroom door closed with a bang, a signal that the kidnapper had left the room in a hurry. They emerged into the bedroom to find their breakfast on a tray. There was cereal, a Kellogg's Variety pack, a big jug of milk, sugar in small packets, small cartons of orange juice with straws attached, slices of toast in a rack with a number of small wrapped pats of butter and a jar of marmalade. Two empty glasses seemed to indicate they should have milk as a drink as well as on their cereal. Some milk had slopped over from the jug to the tray, confirming the haste with which he had left the room when Julie had screamed out.

They were both hungry, although the kidnapper was seeing to their material needs well enough, they had been upset and frightened and had not really eaten properly the previous day despite their liking the food that had been delivered to them. Now, though they remained frightened, hunger won and they both ate all the breakfast provided. Both chose a sugary cereal which they would not have had on offer at home.

"It's light outside now," said Jake, echoing Julie's earlier thought, "maybe someone will see our flag."

"I said that already you know." After Julie's response they lapsed into silence. Neither of them held out great hopes for the flag, knowing that where it was located made it at best a long shot. In due course the collection routine was repeated and the breakfast tray taken away. No note was left behind. Jake made his usual check on the door and, as usual, it was locked.

The security screen covering the window prevented them seeing down onto the area at the back of the house, but they had worked out that they could tell when the kidnapper came and went by the sound of the car starting up and driving out. This morning, after he had collected their breakfast tray, they had heard sounds that indicated that the car had been driven away likely leaving them alone in the house.

"I think he's gone" said Julie. This set Jake thinking.

"We've only seen him, but there could be more than one person." Julie let out a cross between a groan and a sigh, she liked the thought that he was gone, not that someone else, some totally unknown someone, might be lurking downstairs. They did not talk about it but they were both still scared that they would be hurt, or worse.

"Come on," said Jake "we have to do something, let's play Uno again." He got the cards out as he spoke and dealt out seven cards to them each. They began to play but also kept an eye on the television which he had left switched on. The programme had changed and a different presenter was now demonstrating making something from a pile of everyday bits and bobs laid out on the table in front of her. Her voice was somewhat unnatural: over the top bright and cheerful.

"What have we got then?" She lifted things in turn. "A plastic bottle, a cotton reel, the cardboard centre of a toilet roll…" The list went on. Jake found himself distracted and wrongly put down a red seven.

"We're on blue Jake, not red." It seemed Julie's mind was more on the game than his was.

"Wait a sec, listen." He focussed on what was showing on the television as the presenter continued to list various items; that done the presenter, who was wearing multi-coloured dungarees covered in spots, went on to actually start making something.

"Right, let's see what we can do - we'll start with a large sheet of paper." As she held up a sheet of blue paper, laid it out and began to fold it, Jake jumped up.

"I may have an idea." He had checked the door when they had come out of the bathroom to find their breakfast delivered. Unsurprisingly it had again been locked, as it had again after the tray had been collected. Now he went and tried it again, though he had no expectation of finding it other than still locked. Then he bent down and looked through the keyhole. He could see nothing beyond the door, this time the key had been left in the lock.

"He's left the key in the lock, we need paper and sticky tape." Julie looked puzzled.

"What for, what are you going to do?"

"Wait and see, I may have an idea."

"You said that, but what? What are you doing?" Jake took no notice and made no immediate reply, he moved the Uno cards aside and got out some A4 sheets from the folder they had found in the room.

"We need a big sheet, help me stick some of these together." He took up the roll of Sellotape that had also been provided and began to stick two sheets together. He shushed Julie when she continued to ask what was going on; he was not sure that his idea would work and if it did then he wanted it to be a surprise. Besides he did not dare get her hopes up, or his own. She began to help and after a few minutes they had six sheets fastened together to make one large one. Jake took the sheet and dropped in onto the floor by the door, smoothing it flat, then he returned to the store of things that had been left to keep them occupied, he came back with a paint brush. He gingerly put the handle end into the lock. It was too large and he changed it for a smaller one.

"Right, the idea is that the paper goes under the door." He smoothed the paper out again and slid it under the door positioning it at the side of the door with the handle and lock on it and twisted it a little to one side.

"Then I'm going to try to push the key out so that it lands on the paper and we can pull it back into the room." He put the brush in the lock and pushed, not too hard, but with what he judged was sufficient force to make it work. He took his time and the key moved just a little. He pushed some more until after what seemed like an age the key had moved sufficiently; it dropped to the floor and they heard it give out a rapid double slap suggesting that it had bounced. His heart beating faster at the sound Jake rapidly bent down and looked through the keyhole again. He stood back up.

"It's on the paper, but only just, it's near the edge... I'll have to be very careful." He knelt down again and began to edge the paper back into the bedroom, pausing every now and then to look through the keyhole, though as the key got nearer to the door it became impossible to see.

"What's going on? Tell me. Is it working?" Julie stood behind him unable to see whether any positive progress was being made.

"I think it's working, it's quite a large key so it's heavy. It's staying put on the paper." He pulled a little more and finally the key was hard against the door, but the gap between the door and the carpet was a little too narrow and the key would not come through into the room.

"It's stuck. I need you to help Julie." He explained the problem and told Julie what to do. He continued with his paper pulling while she flattened the carpet just below the door to increase the size of the gap.

"Be very gentle." They both held their breath and, after a second or two the end of the key was just visible below the door. Julie pressed down on it and drew it into the room. They looked at each other and Jake could see Julie drawing breath to shout.

"Shhh, shhh! There may still be someone else downstairs." He took the key from her and put it in the lock, turned it with care and it gave a soft click and unlocked. He opened the door an inch and peeped out, seeing just the empty landing, he put an ear to the gap and listened. He could hear nothing.

"Can we go now?" Julie's whispered question sounded plaintive, but Jake offered only another "Shhh!"

He continued to listen for a few more moments, but there was no sound, the house remained completely silent.

"I can't hear anything. Come on. But no noise, okay?" Julie nodded at him her face betraying her relief and excitement but also uncertainty, they both realised that the kidnapper could return at any moment or that there might indeed be a second person somewhere in the house. If so they could find themselves locked up again in a moment. Jake opened the door wide and led the way, they crept down the stairs, pausing every couple of steps to listen. They heard nothing until one step gave out a loud creak prompting a sharp intake of breath from them both. They stopped dead in their tracks and remained unmoving for a moment. Nothing happened, the silence continued and it still appeared that, for the moment, they were alone in the house. They went down the last few steps and reached the hall, but when Jake tried to open the front door he found it locked. Turning the other way they went through to the kitchen where they discovered that the back door, although locked, had a key in it. Jake opened it up. They were out of the room and out of the house, they were free.

"Wait a minute." Julie grabbed her brother's arm.

"What? Come on, we have to go."

"We should take the bikes, I don't want to leave them - I want to keep my new one."

"There's no time. We have to get out, come on, he may come back any minute." When Jake got no reply he turned round and saw that Julie was already back at the bottom of the stairs and starting upwards. Huffing under his breath he turned, followed her and decided not to argue.

"Alright, but quickly, very quickly!" They rushed up the stairs, heedless now of the noise they made and came back down with the bikes clattering alongside them. A moment later they were outside the back door.

"Oh, it's cold" said Julie as soon as they were out into the December morning air. They had no coats to put on having gone from the library straight into a car.

"But we're out, and you were right, we can use the bikes to get right away from the house. Hang on, we should still be quiet." In the silence that followed they both heard the unmistakeable sound of footsteps and voices coming along the path at the side of the house.

"Quick we must hide," whispered Jake. Right next to them on the other side of the path as they stood just outside the back door was an old wooden garage, Jake was standing by its side door and he quickly pushed it open and wheeled his bike inside, Julie followed and he pulled the door closed behind them signalling again for her to be quiet. A moment later the sound of footsteps ceased. Then they heard a crash, the sound of breaking glass and low indistinct voices. They stood rigid and cold wondering both what was going on and what they should do next. They waited, trying not to move, until after some minutes of silence Jake whispered that they should make a run for it. No sooner had he spoken and turned his bike round to point to the door than there was the unmistakable sound of the back door opening just outside. After a few moments further sounds seemed to indicate that it had been closed again. Someone was definitely there, now by the sound of it inside the house, it seemed either the kidnapper was back or that he had an accomplice. Whoever was in the house was about to discover that the children had gone. They waited some more, hearing no more, then Jake whispered.

"I can't hear anything, now may be our only chance. Let's go. Listen: I'll open the door, we then wheel the bikes out, get on a pedal like mad. Okay?"

CHAPTER TWENTY ONE
A very special Santa Claus

That morning while Jake and Julie were still locked up securely in the house their abductor had rented he was busy going about executing the next bit of his plan. He had a short journey to make. He had issued the ransom demand and now knew it had been received and would, he believed, be acted upon. In his note he had asked that the words "Will do" be added at the top of the Home page of the Demonaxx corporate web site to signify agreement to comply with his instructions and when he had duly clicked onto the site he had seen that it appeared there. Kent had doubtless not added the words in himself, he doubted that he would have known how, but whoever he had instructed to do so had put them in brackets on a line above the normal start line; the entry was in small type. Any other people visiting the opening page of the site might puzzle over it for a split second before ignoring it; more likely they would not even notice it. He felt that this showed that he had reached a pivotal moment in his plan and he had sat for a moment at his computer taking it all in before coming out of the web site.

So, he knew the money should be delivered.

He had spent some time giving this stage careful thought. He reckoned that Kent was a particularly busy man, he was under pressure, he had a role heading up a large company, a company under considerable extra pressure from the media and public because of the row about the price of their cancer drug; furthermore the man was now faced with a major threat to his nearest and dearest. One day recently he had followed him to Witham railway station early in the morning, then checked again in the evening, the car was still there at 9.3o; he was working late in the office despite the fact that his wife at home was coping with their children currently being on holiday. He reckoned that if he asked for a reasonable amount of money Kent would just pay up aiming to see the whole thing ended fast. He was gambling on him not reporting the ransom details to the police, at least not early on. In one sense making that assumption had been a huge risk, but he had thought he knew enough about Kent to judge that this would be highly likely to be his reaction. If all did not go well, he would still regard it as having been worth a go and the payment of money was, after all, not the only thing he was aiming to achieve. Even if he was caught he might well achieve something. But what would a man such as Kent, with such a large and profitable company to call on, regard as a reasonable sum, a sum that could be produced in cash fast, without any hassle or too many awkward questions being asked? This was a difficult one. He had thought long and hard about it, and decided that the sum of £100,000 seemed about right. Surely, he thought, this would be regarded as small change for a man in Kent's position, but a very decent sum for his own purposes. Besides in the used notes he had specified to be delivered a greater sum would simply be too bulky and heavy.

He had intentionally kept the timeline short, aiming not to give Kent time to think anything other than "get it done" and he saw the response appearing on the web site without any delay as a good sign. Certainly good enough to move on to the next stage. He was committed now and had specified that the money was to be handed over in the centre of Chelmsford and he set up off to drive there in good time as morning traffic into the town was always heavy. He did not want the whole plan foundering on a traffic jam on the road into town: the so called Army & Navy roundabout was notorious for hold ups. On most occasions if he visited Chelmsford he used the park and ride service, completing the journey on the special buses that ran into the town centre from car parks on the edge every ten minutes.

He had parked his car as near as possible to the central area of the town. It was market day and the traffic free area in the centre of the shopping area was busy with a variety of stalls set up selling everything from fruit and vegetables to blinds and curtains already open and trading. Timing was important, he did not want to hang about in a way that might draw attention to himself for any longer than necessary. His instructions specified that the money should to be delivered at 11 a.m. sharp.

He stopped by the small clock tower in the central pedestrian-only street to find it busy with shoppers going to and fro along a stretch of street well decorated for Christmas. Coloured lights flashed on and off and a little further up the street a small group of musicians were playing carols and seasonal songs. The area had not just shops but also a variety of market stalls in the area just beyond him, and it was largely these that created a hurly burly scene where shoppers were unlikely to remember any one small detail as they busied themselves with their own missions. He had arrived with maybe a couple of minutes to spare and, just as he had instructed, he was approached almost at once by a man carrying two large shopping bags – bags for life, how appropriate that was he thought. In his ransom note he had arranged a password for them to exchange.

"Good morning special Santa Claus," said the man doing the delivery.

"Yes, very special" he replied.

The brief exchange over, nothing more was said, the man put the bags down at his feet and walked on – again just as he had been instructed. He appeared undistinguished: maybe forty years old, he wore a green padded jacket and jeans and would be difficult to recall. Anyway the man was gone in a moment, quickly disappearing amongst the crowds of shoppers leaving him free to continue with the plan.

His own two red sacks contained a small number of gift wrapped parcels, but were still amply large enough for his purpose. Inside the shopping bags were a number of separately wrapped packages, he had asked for this as it made the money transfer more manageable. He took them out and put them into his sacks, placing them below the Christmas packages, which would be all that could be seen if anyone looked in the bags, although this was something he did not regard as likely. He forced his hands to move at a brisk pace as he made the transfer, balancing things so that the two bags weighed much the same. They were a good deal heavier now than when he arrived. Stuffing the shopping bags into a litter bin as he went, he then headed back in the direction of his car.

The man who had delivered the money had been briefed by James Kent not only to make the delivery but to follow the man to whom the delivery was made and telephone the location of where he went to Kent. He had worked for the company for some fifteen years, involved in maintaining the building, but had also done a variety of chores for James Kent over the years, some of them personal, all of them involving privacy. He knew nothing of the present circumstances, nothing about the children, nor the fact that the packages contained enough money to perhaps challenge his loyalties. The substantial tip he always got for carrying out any such chore meant that he was happy to just do as he was told. The man watched from behind the window of McDonalds as his quarry walked away. The jacket he was wearing was reversible, he had turned it from green to brown and put on a flat cap. It was unlikely that his quarry would spot him. He kept a safe distance and followed along in a direction that appeared to be heading towards the nearest car park, his quarry crossed the road and went into an open area of the car park situated partly below a flyover and then on into a multi-story. Kent's man had guessed right, anyone picking up two heavy bags would want to park as near as possible to the collection point to avoid too long a walk; his own car was nearby, parked there on the very same premise.

Still keeping his distance the man watched as the two sacks were put into the boot of a car and his quarry climbed into the driving seat, started the car and headed for the exit. To be thorough the man scribbled down the registration number. Few people were currently leaving the car park, it was the time of day when most of the people around were still arriving and heading for the shops; despite the power of the internet shopping areas were full of Christmas shoppers, albeit some were doubtless just browsing and would buy elsewhere. Now as he followed behind in his own car he hung back just a little watching as a hand came out of the window of the car ahead and put a ticket into the machine. The barrier lifted. He began to follow, but another car pulled in front of him from the side. Fine he thought, one won't hurt, shouldn't get too close anyway, though he was confident he would not be recognised and could catch up once both cars were clear of the car park.

Then he saw that once his quarry's car had driven through the raised barrier it had not driven away, but stopped at once. The Father Christmas clad figure jumped out, took a couple of quick steps back and appeared to put another ticket into the machine, he returned at once to his car and drove off. The single car now between him and the ticket machine was driven by a woman with a crying infant in the back, she moved forward, put her ticket in without looking at the machine which was flashing a notice saying "Error. Press bell for assistance". When at last she noticed that the normal barrier opening procedure was not working, she had to get out of the car to reach the call button. Sorting this out was clearly going to take some time.

As the figure still dressed as Father Christmas drove away he could see a young woman getting out of her car behind him. Though he had been reasonably certain Kent would not contact the police with the ransom details he had also been pretty sure that he would have arranged for him to be followed. What father would not want to find out where his children were being held and apprehend whoever had taken them? On a previous visit to the car park he had summoned assistance and claimed to have lost his ticket. It had taken a few minutes of slow moving officialdom to get out, he had then kept the "lost" ticket and used it today finding that an out of date ticket had gummed up the works just as he had hoped. Long before any follower could be on his tail he had been heading out of the town and there was no clue left as to the direction he had taken. He kept moving but took care to do so carefully and not break the speed limit.

He was soon back safely at his own house and put the car away in his garage. It had a door into the house so there was no way anyone could see him unload his sacks. With the main part of his plan apparently completed successfully there was no sign of his having been spotted or of any kind of pursuit. Unbeknown to him, James Kent's aide, having had to report that his attempt at tailing whoever had collected the bags had resulted in failure would later check the number plate he had written down, finding details of the registered owner and an address in Maldon. Making a visit there he had discovered only that the car belonged to an elderly lady whose neighbours reported was currently in hospital; he knew it would take more than that to restore James Kent's faith in him.

With the money in his hands the plan left only a few details to take care of, including the matter of the children.

CHAPTER TWENTY TWO

Nearly there

I'm lying flat on my back in what was once a flower bed with the breath knocked out of me and I can't move. As my wits return I realise that I have been run into by a bicycle, it is that holding my legs down and what I quickly also realise is that Jake is sprawled alongside me and across my legs. I am not sure which of us is the most surprised. As I look up I see that Julie is sitting astride a bright blue bike a step or two further back, I can see too that she seems to recognise us, but I need to be sure, we don't want to frighten them.

"Hey, you two, remember us, it's Alice and Margaret from the library. I'm Alice," I say this as both Jake and I struggle up in a tangle of limbs and Julie says simply, "Yes." She gives a broad smile that is probably as much relief to see some friendly faces as it is pleasure to see us two again. Perhaps it's a bit of both.

"Were you in this house, did you escape?" This time it's Jake who speaks up.

"Yes, we were… we were locked up, but I got the key. Yes." His words tumble out in an untidy rush.

"This way, quick now. Let's get you away from here and into the car," I turn and lead the way down the drive towards the Mini. "We need to get you away from here right now." To have found the kids is astounding, but I imagine it all coming tumbling down as some heavy with a gun appears and we all four get locked up. I walk a few steps down the drive towards the car assuming that the kids are following right behind me, but when I glance back to be sure they are hanging back.

"What's the matter, get a move on, whoever took you may come back."

"Can we bring the bikes, they are ours aren't they? It's what the man promised us." I was right about the Father Christmas's suit then. It seemed clear now that it was definitely used as both a ruse to draw the kids away and as a disguise. I am loath to delay us getting away from here, but why the heck not. I presume the kids have had a tough time, I reckon the very least they deserve is a new bike; besides they are right there.

"Okay Julie, but come *quickly*." Jake grabs his bike and pushes it quickly ahead, Julie is still astride the other one and simply pushes the pedals and they follow me towards the car. Margaret is glancing ahead of us down the road, there's a car coming along it towards us, it appears empty apart from the driver, who's a man, the car gets nearer and nearer. Then, before we can panic, it turns into the driveway of another house. The driver gets out, does not even glance at us, and goes inside via his front door. I open up the back doors of the Mini, there should just about be room to house the bikes. I lean in and undo the release clips and fold the back seats down. As the kids catch up I take the first bike and put it inside, then the next goes in on top, one blue, one red. They fit but, with the back seats folded down, there's no proper room for the children.

"Jake, can you climb on top here somehow? Be quick." I take off my anorak and spread it out to give him some protection from any sharp edges on the bike. Jake scrambles in largely on top, he lies on his stomach looking ahead. No problem, he's sorted. I shut the doors.

"Okay, Margaret, can you get in and take Julie on your lap somehow?" They organise that while I move round the car and get into the driver's seat thinking that we are going to arrive at the police station without all the seat belts being properly fastened. Sod it, we need to leave right now. I turn the key and the engine fails to start. I try it again. It can be a pig in the cold weather. In the mirror I see another car heading down the cul de sac towards us. The engine fires on the third try and I turn at once into the nearest drive and reverse around to retrace our steps back down the road. In my haste I crash the gear, but then we are underway. I concentrate on driving and note in the mirror that the other car has turned into a drive, it's not the kidnapper. I ask if everyone's okay and both kids say they are fine. They can't be comfortable, but they are free – and we don't have far to go. A thought strikes me as I turn into Arcacia Avenue. I pull into the kerb and stop. I pull on the handbrake and turn in my seat.

"I am so sorry you two, we didn't really ask properly, now tell me - are you really okay?" They both say yes simultaneously then Jake tells us.

"It was horrid, at first he seemed nice, he told us about the bikes, but then he locked us in."

"It was scary," added Julie. "But Jake got us out; can we go home now?" Two more questions:

"Did he hurt you in any way, any way at all?" I should have addressed this much sooner, maybe our destination should be a hospital, however they both say a firm no, then Jake adds a little more.

"He never came in the room, he made us go in the bathroom when he brought us food." One more question, then we will get going.

"Did you see who it was, his face?" Julie speaks up first.

"No, only the Santa Claus suit and the big white beard." As Jake agrees with this there is a fierce tapping on the kerbside window right next to Margaret's head. We all jump and my first thought is that the kidnapper has caught up with us, but alongside the car stands a smartly dressed middle aged woman wearing a maroon beret, she speaks in a booming voice.

"What do you two think you are doing? Those children aren't safe, they need seat belts on." I let out a sigh of relief that it is nothing that poses a danger, but Margaret speaks up at once. She has slid the window back an inch or two.

"They are very much safer than they were a few minutes ago. We've just rescued them from a kidnapper, next stop the police station." The woman's face is a picture. She starts to say something but I interrupt her.

"Read all about it in the local paper!" I shout as I put the car in gear and we set off again. I turn right and am then on the main road heading in towards the town centre.

"Margaret's right, we are only a little way from the police station now, I think we should take you there. You'll be safe there. Everyone's been looking for you, your parents were so worried." Well, your mother was, I had not seen or heard about James Kent at all. What an unworthy thought, but I really didn't take to the man. Jake acknowledges that this makes sense with an "Okay", then he poses a question.

"How did you find us, did you see the flag?" Margaret begins to explain.

"We did see the flag, that's how we knew we were in the right place, but we tracked you down to the house with your watch." For a second in the mirror I see Jake glance at his wrist and put on a puzzled look.

"How did you do that?"

"It's a long story, we'll tell you later, look, we are nearly there."

While they have been speaking I have got to the roundabout at the top of the town and now take the second turning to the left to the police station, then realise almost at once that it has moved recently, the old building in front of us is all boarded up and taking a while to find a new owner. The new location is alongside the local Council offices at the other end of town. Pure habit and, if I am honest, a little bit of over excitement, but my excuse is that I have been in the town only a few months. It was budget cuts: the police and the Council swore that the new location was just as good, perhaps a better situation in fact, but residents mostly think having no police station in the town centre is a bad thing and I'm inclined to agree with them. Maldon is not a huge town, but it still gets some anti-social behaviour going on especially on a Saturday night. I apologise and explain what I am doing as I turn the car round and ask Margaret to phone the police station so that they know we are on our way. I am aching to find out how the kids managed to escape, but for the moment this is more important: I get my mobile phone out of my pocket.

"Dialling 999's no good, that goes to Chelmsford I think. Use my phone, it has Sergeant Jane's number in the list of contacts. Look under P for police." That is quickly found and it takes only a moment for Margaret to get through to her.

"Sergeant Jane? ... This is Margaret, you know from the library, yes, yes, I'm with Alice Carter from the local newspaper. We're in her car. We have the children… yes, yes… yes, *those* children. We found them, Julie and Jake, they both seem fine… No, not hurt. We are not far away, we'll be at the police station in four or five minutes. We'll explain then." She listens for a moment more, says "Okay" and cuts the connection.

"There you go kids, now they are expecting you and your Mum is there waiting. Look we're nearly there."

Two minutes later we turn into the area in front of the Council offices, miraculously there is a visitor space free. I park, get out and open the back doors of the car to let Jake scramble out, the others get out too and we turn towards the station entrance to find Sergeant Jane standing at the doorway. She calls something over her shoulder into the building and there is immediately quite a reception committee coming out of the door, some in uniform, some not. Elizabeth Kent runs ahead of them all and the kids run up to and hug her. She looks haggard and has tears running down her face, but I imagine that these are now tears of relief and joy.

I am happy for them, and I can also see the potential headline more clearly now: "Reporter and Librarian find missing children". Or is the word "rescue" better? The dictionary says rescue is to "save or set free, bring away from attack, custody, danger or harm". Hmm, I need to bear in mind that the kids themselves escaped; maybe "Escaping kidnapped kids brought to safety by local reporter and librarian" is more like it, though at the moment I have no idea how on Earth they managed to get out. Something else I must find out.

CHAPTER TWENTY THREE

Stay in the car

No sooner have the group spilled out of my battered Mini and the children have been reunited with their parents than the initial response of the police becomes very apparent. Inspector Stuart strides over and poses us an immediate key question.

"Where did you find them? Do you know where they were kept captive?" Now this is a real opportunity. The children are safe, I need to speak to them, to get their full story, but this is important too. I think fast about how I can use the moment. If I get this right it will add so much to the story, my story. Right, I know how to answer.

"Yes, we found the house they were held in, it's here in Maldon, not so far away. But I didn't even notice the name of the road – I can show you though." He immediately directs the same enquiry to Margaret, his bluntness signifying the urgency.

"What about you?" Margaret shakes her head and answers with a simple "no", I wonder if she has sussed out my intentions. The look on the Inspector's face says no way, but only for a second, he clearly thinks that having a reporter along is very much not the best thing ever but there's an urgency too, they need to go there right now, and I guess he is well aware of that.

"Okay, come on – but you have to do as you're told." Yes. Mission accomplished. He signals to Sergeant Jane and leads the way towards a nearby police car, shouting over his shoulder to someone behind him to organise others to follow. The Sergeant drives, the Inspector gets in the passenger seat beside her and I quickly climb into the back before he has time to change his mind. I start to give directions.

"Okay, first drive to the Queen Victoria pub, you know the one just before you get to the bypass." Sergeant Jane says that she know it and we head off.

"Did you see anyone, any sign of weapons, were the children hurt in any way?" I guess the Inspector wants to know what they are likely to find when they get there. As do we all.

"We didn't see anyone, and no, certainly no weapons, as far as I could gather from the kids they were well cared for – well, apart from being kidnapped and locked up that is. Once they got to the house I don't think they ever saw him again. The house is not fully furnished, I imagine it was used just for this, so I suspect he was not there all the time, maybe he only went into the house to deliver food. And Jake told me that he got them to go in a bathroom while he did that." I resist saying any more about the house at this stage.

"Okay we'll see." We are now at the roundabout at the top of the High Street, Sergeant Jane puts out a brief burst on the siren, I can see the flashing blue lights above our heads reflected in the bonnet and in a shop window alongside us, other traffic slows and she is allowed to drive straight across. She's setting a brisk pace and we are now approaching the pub, which is visible ahead of us on the right. We are on it very fast and I nearly leave it too late to indicate that we should now turn.

"You take a left here, down Arcacia Avenue, then slow down - I don't know the area and need to find the next turning. It was on the

140

right." She slows a little, though the tyres still squeal for a second as we take the corner, then she slows right down and we drive slowly past the entrance to Norfolk Road. A little further on, there it is, I recognise the turning.

"Now, now, take the next right. The road's a dead end, it only goes maybe half a mile, and the house we want is right at the end and faces this way down the road towards us. There are doors front and back, but I don't think there's a way out of the small garden at the back. There's an old wooden garage too, that's out of sight behind the house." The police car draws up at the kerb. We are about thirty feet short of the house. A second police car, which has been following close behind us draws up alongside us so that it's positioned in a way that blocks the road.

"You. Stay in the car." The Inspector directs this remark to me over his shoulder in a clipped tone as he and his colleagues get out of the cars and begin to move forward. For the moment I don't move, his voice suggests that he would brook no argument, and I let his instruction lie. They are all keeping quiet and no sirens were used as they approached nearer to the location. If the kidnapper has returned to the house and gone inside since we left then he may well not know what's happening. Well. Not. Yet. The police spread out, one starts to go down the side path to the left, another to go to the right and round towards the back and the garage, the others are now at the front door, one is holding a metal battering ram and as I start to get out – there was no way was I ever just going to sit there throughout the piece observing from a distance - he whacks the door just below the lock. It's old and wooden and flies straight open on the first blow, the frame splinters. There was never any way I was going to stay in the car, no way at all, I hurry up the front path; everyone is looking the other way, towards the house, and I'm sure none of them is giving me a single thought.

Someone shouts: "Police. Police. Don't move." They are inside now. I close on them from behind and at the front door I find everyone has gone further into the house, warning shouts continue to come from further away, and I can walk into the hall unhindered. I already know that the room in which the kids were held is upstairs. As shouts of "All clear" now echo around the place replacing the warnings, I slip up the stairs taking them two at a time. It appears the house is empty. A police constable is standing on the top step, I arrive behind him just as he turns to come down and I turn sideways, slip past him and take a step or two further on towards the bedroom.

"Hey you. Stop right there. What do you think you're doing? This is a crime-scene!" He sounds very threatening, I wonder if having a voice that carries extreme authority is a standard part of the police job description. I do stop, it won't help my case to get arrested, but I'm at the bedroom door and I have a clear view inside. Thinking of the headline, perhaps "Inside the children's prison", I take a slow look round as a heavy hand falls on my shoulder and I turn away and am ushered down the stairs. The hand does not leave my shoulder, and the strong grip is maintained until we are back downstairs in the hall. The Inspector is standing by the front door. He looks stern in a way that reminds me of a cross school teacher faced with dumb insolence from an errant pupil.

"I thought I told you to stay in the car." I barely glanced at the room previously now I can add a good deal of detail, and having got what I wanted I think I can afford to be bold.

"Sorry, yes, I know. On the other hand I did find the children and lead you here. I think a thank you might be in order, you know, and one for Margaret too." He doesn't answer me, he's pointing, indicating I should leave, I go out of the house and make my way back down the front path towards the cars. I catch the word "forensics" in what is being said behind me and see more police have now arrived in a third car and a plastic ribbon "police line" is being strung across the front of the house. I imagine the investigation here will take some time.

I am driven back to the police station and I am told I should make a statement before I leave. I can't wait to get back to the office, I have a story to write – a big one - though I am already wondering just how much of it Smaug will let me write up myself. The police are adamant about the statement, and details are understandably needed now. Leaving is not an option just yet. Margaret and I sit down together and go through our tale. We are in a drab little room not much more than three or four metres square, furnished only with a table and chairs all of which have seen better days. We should be the heroes of the hour and surely deserve a bit more comfort, it's not the sort of surroundings to encourage a cosy chat. Nevertheless I begin to tell the tale.

"Margaret started it, she gave me Jake's bag to return and I read the instructions for the watch." This only gets only a puzzled look, so I go back a bit.

"The children each got a prize for their stories in the library writing competition, it was a book token and a watch for each of them. Jake's is a smart watch, it has a monitor... a sort of tracker thingy on it apparently designed to send details of the wearer's location out so that it can be picked up on a mobile phone; I think it's designed as a safety feature for kids. He's probably still wearing it on his wrist. You can have a look."

"Why didn't you tell anyone?" The inevitable question. No surprise there. Well, because I wanted *us* to find them and for that to give me my big story, that's why, but of course, I don't say that. Margaret sees the problem and gives me a glance that suggests she should answer this one.

"We weren't even sure of exactly what it did or how to operate it; I'm not very technical. We found it needed an app, Alice downloaded that and we were working it out as we went along. Even when we got to what we thought was the house we weren't sure, we could have been wrong or it could have been somewhere else nearby. We started to check it out and saw a flag the children had managed to hang out at the back of the house. The word 'Help' on that showed that it was the right place. Then the children found us, they had escaped. We don't know how they did that yet." Okay, now I can join in.

"They took the bikes." This gets another blank look so I explain. "The kidnapper was dressed as Father Christmas and lured them out of the library by telling them that there was another prize, a bike for each of them. And there really were bikes in the house. When the kids somehow got out, they took the bikes with them and we discovered them because Jake ran into me as he cycled round the back corner of the house. He sent me flying, I've still got the bruises."

"Well, we'll be talking to the children too of course, but you saw no sign of the perpetrator?" My turn again:

"No, no sign at all."

"Anything else you can add, anything that might help?" I realise I have to come clean about searching the house, if only because my fingerprints must be everywhere and might confuse things and, my news story apart, the last thing I want to do is to confuse their investigation.

"Yes, I suppose there is. You will find my fingerprints inside the house." The Inspector looks set to interrupt, but I plough resolutely on, choosing my words with some care. "A window at the side of the house was broken, I could reach in and open it so that I could climb in. Margaret kept watch as we were not sure whether the kidnapper was in the house or not. I just nipped quickly round and, as you know, the children were not there. We then discovered their escape as we went to the back of the house to check the garage." I see no need to explain exactly how the window got broken. I am pretty sure that saying anything more would prompt the thought that we had broken it intentionally.

"I am not sure that I approve of that, not at all, if someone had been there in the house we might be dealing with you as hostages as well." He pauses giving me a long hard look before adding: "Or something worse."

"Yes, well, I suppose so, but all's well that ends well surely and the main thing is that the kids are safe." I try to treat what I had done dismissively but also to look suitably chastened by his remark. I am not sure that I succeed in either regard and I reckon he would be much more critical if I had done what I did and the children had not been found. He organises a constable to take my fingerprints and doing that takes a while longer, though it's an interesting process, one carried out with considerable precision. As I clean my hands afterwards I wonder how long my identity will be kept on file, but it does not seem to be the moment to ask such a question. Anyway for however long I am "on file" I better be well behaved. The significance of our role was perhaps considerable, but the details we know of what went on previously are actually very few. I don't think anything we saw or did will make the job of catching the perpetrator any easier. It is not as if we faced down a ruthless gangster or fought them off with our bare hands. Margaret waited while I was "inked" and that done we are allowed to go on our way. We see no sign of the Kents or their children as we go, maybe they have been taken home, if I want to speak to them again, and of course I do, then I am going to have to get in touch.

As we walk back towards the car we hear a shout behind us.

"Hang a moment please you two." We turn to see a police constable is hurrying after us. He catches up with us and continues.

"Sorry, ladies, we forgot about the bikes. They are evidence and we must hang onto them. Fingerprints and so on." In some ways it's a reasonable request, I have just had my prints taken after all, but Margaret isn't having it.

"No, you can't possibly do that. The children have been promised those bikes, don't you think they've been through enough?" The policeman looks a little uncomfortable.

"I am afraid it's not possible, evidence is evidence, I'm sorry, but that's how it is." Margaret is not giving up.

"Then I think we need to see the Inspector please." She turns and starts to walk back towards the police station. I am impressed with her stand and join in.

"If it's that important then go and get him. We'll wait here." Margaret stops, we both stare at him and after a brief pause he returns inside. A few minutes later we are speaking with the Inspector who comes out with the same constable.

"We just don't think this is fair to the children, we...." Margaret starts the exchange but is interrupted almost at once.

"You have a fair point and we all feel so much for those kids, but we have to take fingerprints, every bit of evidence is important. You do want us to catch whoever did this don't you?" The question is clearly rhetorical as he continues right on. "I will personally guarantee to get this sorted within a day or two and have the bikes delivered to the children at their home – they will have them well before Christmas then. But I suggest we check with the Kents first, it may seem a good thing for the kids to keep them, but it's just possible that having them might bring back bad memories. What do you think?" I look at Margaret and she looks at me.

"Okay, your point about checking with the parents seems sensible, I hadn't thought of that. Okay Margaret?" She readily agrees and I get the bikes out of the car and prop one up on its stand as the constable, now wearing protective gloves takes the other.

"Margaret hasn't touched them and you have my prints, we'll leave it with you and I would be grateful if you can tell me if and when they go back to the children, it may rate a mention in a future story."

We say our goodbyes and now we're again in the Mini on our way back to the town centre. Margaret's thinking ahead.

"You know what, I was only supposed to be on a short break. Some break. They will think I've done a runner."

"Me too, but it was all in a good cause. Don't worry, if Philip complains just refer him to me. You can tell him one of his staff is going to get some really good publicity in the next local paper. It will reflect well on the library. We should get together later. Do you want a bite to eat together this evening?"

"Sure, yes, that would be nice, I'll give you a ring."

I park up back in the car park, Margaret heads off towards the library giving me a wave as she goes and then I'm rushing down the High Street and back to the office, where no doubt Smaug has noticed my prolonged absence and is all ready to read me the riot act.

CHAPTER TWENTY FOUR

Is that a story?

Back in the office, I say hello to Becky as I walk in, she looks up at the clock and makes an exaggerated tut tutting noise as I pass. Yes, I suppose I have been out quite a while. I have only been sat in my cubicle for a matter of seconds before the editorial summons comes; I have not even had time to check for messages or look at my latest "to do" list. He must have seen me come in through that glass wall of his.

"Alice, where the hell have you been? Get in here will you." I sigh and head to Smaug's lair, move one file to create an empty chair and sit down opposite his desk. I realise he knows nothing of what's been happening and I have been gone for some hours.

"You've been out for hours, what goes on?" I reckon if I launch straight into it, he may in fact listen.

"You know the kidnapped children, well…" But he is interrupting before I can even begin to get started.

"Yes, yes, John's on that story, I've got other things for you to…" This time it's me doing the interrupting, I need to get enough of it out to make him listen.

"Hang on, give me a moment. The kids, you know *the* kids… they are out, released. Free and unharmed. What's more it was me that found them." I allow myself a tiny pause during which he looks stunned and is quiet for sufficiently long for me to get in another sentence.

"Well, Margaret – you know from the library – and I – we tracked them down. I have just come back from making a statement at the police station, that's where we took them. I had my fingerprints taken. Now is that a story, or is that a story?"

"Well, that's... that's quite a surprise. Okay... you better tell me all about it then." I have never known him to be quiet for so long, but he is, he lets me go through the whole thing, well the highlights, including the fact that I had seen, and can describe, the room the kids were held in. I pause and he says nothing for a long moment, then he asks a question that surprises and puzzles me.

"How long have you been here Alice?" Now what's he going on about? I think for a split second.

"I got back about twenty minutes ago, why?"

"No, how long have you worked here?" Okay, but I still don't know where he's going with this.

"Must be almost six months, I think, why on Earth?" Okay, now what?

"Well this seems to have come at just about the right time. This will be your story, I want a page, at least a page, no, let's say two pages, full pages, for the next edition. Organise some photos – including one of you and Margaret – and the children - don't forget the follow up, talk to the parents, okay? And the kids too, of course. They know you now, right? Then there will no doubt be more to do for next week's issue about the police investigation. Keep in touch with them. Or maybe you will have caught the kidnapper by then, eh?" Do I detect the slight suggestion of a smile as he says that last bit? You know what, I really think I do.

"Yes. Okay. Thanks Bob." A pathetic response. Never mind, it's a result, indeed it's more than I dared to hope for. I sit back in my cubicle hardly able to believe anything that's just happened either out with our search or just now with old Smaug. The man almost seems human, so much so that I may have to reconsider his nickname. I am conscious of someone at my side, I look up and he's come out of his office and is standing alongside my desk, looming over me.

"Go on then, get to work, and talk to John, I'll tell him it must be your story now and get him to brief you as to how to sell your tale on to the nationals. Work together on that, but it should have your name on it. Okay? Go. Go."

Alright. I'm going. I'm going. I remain sitting down, look at my notes, make some more and then start typing. It will be the most important piece I have written to date. Before I get very far I have to pause to liaise with John about the nationals, all useful stuff, but I itch to get back to my writing.

By five o'clock I am the only one in the office, my rumbling stomach reminds me that I've had no lunch. I take a break and go over the road to Costa and get a muffin and a coffee to take out; hang the expense, I need to fuel this task and work on without distraction. Back at my desk I take a further moment to text Margaret, she replies and we have an arrangement to meet at seven o'clock for a drink. I resume my typing and work on a while longer. By the time I leave I'm pleased: I reckon I have a fair draft, something I can check over in the morning and which will hopefully not need too much editing after I have slept on it overnight. I note where an up to date quote from the police must go in later, click on save, shut down the computer and lock up as I leave the office.

*

I am a few minutes late meeting Margaret, who is already sitting in the bar at the Blue Boar Hotel at the top of the High Street in the old world charm of which an open fire keeps it cosy. She is nursing a glass of white wine.

"Hi, sorry I'm late I couldn't leave what I was writing about today's events in the middle."

"No problem. I bet you need a drink, I know I do." I go to the bar and come back with a glass of lager and a menu.

"I don't know about you, but I got no real lunch today and I'm now more than somewhat peckish." We agree that food is essential, look at the menu and I go back to the bar to order something. Then, now settled, we compare notes, marvelling at how it was Jake's watch that made finding the house possible and expressing relief that we did not come face to face with the kidnapper and that the kids were unharmed.

"They really did seem okay, didn't they, I hope they don't suffer any long term effects, I am sure if it was me I would be having nightmares." I share Margaret's sentiments, then have a thought about reliving my experience.

"I just had a thought. My Mother still follows everything I write, she has a subscription to the Express, and anything interesting she is always on the phone about wanting more details, the conversation about this is going to beat all length records and I bet I will be told we should not have done what we did. What about you? Do you have any regrets?" Margaret explains how she feels.

"Not at all, well at least not now it's all over, in the event the place was empty, I would not have liked to have walked into some heavy with a gun. And it ended well, we got the kids away and they are safe and sound. All good, though I have to confess I had my heart in my mouth more than once, especially when that window broke so noisily."

"Me too. I am glad you backed me up when I told the Inspector about my going into the house, I didn't want him to think we had broken in on purpose." Though I very much expect that, had things been different, that is exactly what I would have done.

"I could see that, Alice, however you got in it was still a risk, I hardly drew breath while you were inside the house." We are quiet for a little while, both I think finding that on reflection, having been carried along in the moment as it all happened, taking it all in as we look back is a somewhat more sobering experience. I tell Margaret that it has been a breakthrough for me at work, that I am going to be able to handle the whole story, at last, and how much that means to me.

"Well, good for you! I think the next issue is one I will want to see, read and keep for a while too. I guess I could send a copy to my

Mum, she's bound to hear about all this and will want chapter and verse."

"Yes, but bear in mind that it will be in the nationals before it's in the weekly local paper, of course, so yes, everyone will see." Before departing and going our separate ways, we change the subject and discuss mothers for a while, we both have mothers who are very supportive and who take an interest in what we do, but who are also rather inclined to fuss a bit too. Neither of us would have it any other way. Mine will doubtless be on the phone tomorrow morning as soon as her morning paper arrives.

CHAPTER TWENTY FIVE
We did it together

The following morning, with the extraordinary events of yesterday still fresh in my mind; I am in the office early. As I walk into what appears to be a still and empty office a phone is ringing, it's on the main incoming line on Becky's desk near the entrance. I pick it up before it prompts the caller to leave a message and announce myself. It's Sergeant Jane.

"Morning Alice. I thought you would be at your office in good time, I don't doubt you have a good deal to write up. That was quite a day yesterday wasn't it?" I concede that it was and she continues.

"Inspector Stuart is going to hold a press conference about this today and wants you to attend and say something about your involvement if you will. It's quite soon - this morning at ten - will that be okay?"

"Yes, of course. Where is it to be held?" I very much want to see my involvement continue as long and as much as possible, so, although I don't look forward to the speaking bit, naturally I am keen to be there.

"I got roped into making all the necessary arrangements, the Inspector's based in Chelmsford and as this is best held here in Maldon it saves another of his team coming over here to fix everything if I make the local arrangements. I thought it might be best held in the library, the children know and like the place and are less likely to be overawed. Philip's agreed to it, and that helped persuade Elizabeth Kent to collaborate and allow the children to be there, and Margaret can attend too. Can you arrive a little before a ten o'clock start? Just to be safe and give us a moment to get organised." It all sound sensible and, given her relationship with Philip, it is hardly surprising that he agreed to the event being held in the library.

"No problem, I'll see you there." I can't wait. I have time to do a few things first and I start by telephoning the Kents.

*

Even at twenty to ten when I arrive I can see that the library is already busy. There is a notice posted on the door explaining what's happening and apologising to regular library users for any disruption to normal service. A crime like this is unusual in Maldon so I don't think many people will think it's inappropriate. A table just inside the front entrance is covered by name badges and is manned by a police constable: he tells me badges are solely for members of the press. I explain that that's me, but he insists that I am here in my capacity as what he calls "a participant in all of this". A number of people from the press seem to have arrived already and I can see some badged individuals are milling about in an area that has been largely cleared in the library's central space, they are clutching what I assume are posh coffees in cardboard cups and, in some cases, cameras. The microphone is back in place, exactly as it was for the prize giving event yesterday at which all this started, and I can see that those I assume are to be involved are now assembling in that area. The Inspector is busy talking to Philip Marchington, Elizabeth is there with the children, both of whom are visibly bubbling with excitement, and Margaret, my partner in crime as it were, is there too. I wave to Elizabeth and the children as Margaret and I greet each other.

"How about this then, Alice? Look what Philip dropped on me as soon as I walked in. I thought it was all over."

"That may well be in some ways, but in my job I rather hope the story isn't all over and has more to it yet. There's a kidnapper to catch, not least." Margaret laughs.

"Yes, certainly is. I really meant that I thought my part in it was all over." We chat for a while, not least to share out which bit of the story we will each describe, then it's time for the Inspector to take charge, as I turn round I see that the room is now quite full. I guess there are at least twenty press people in attendance, who are identified by their name badges, and I notice a couple of regular library users are peeping round shelves to see what is going on. They remind me rather of timid rabbits hesitating before leaving cover and crossing open ground; I can't help wondering if they are in the crime section, but cannot see the signs. Margaret told me that Philip did not want the library closed, just for it to be made clear to members that they had to take a back seat for a while. Fair enough. The Inspector seats us "participants" on a row of chairs set out alongside the microphone, me next to Jake and Elizabeth between him and Julie. He gives it a couple of taps and speaks up. I switch on the record function on my mobile phone.

"Good morning. I'm Inspector Stuart, I'm with the Chelmsford CID and I'm heading up this investigation. Welcome to our friends from the press, the others here are…" He indicates the row of us and lists our names. I am not sure this is his favourite part of the job either, his tone is flat and one might almost think he is uninterested; actually I think the dictionary would rather have me use disinterested, but maybe his voice does not reflect his true feelings; in fact, introduction over, he warms to the task somewhat.

"To say the least, these two youngsters have had a scary time. It started when they won the top prizes in the library's Christmas writing competition for children. At the prize giving here in this room the day before yesterday they were abducted by a man wearing a Father Christmas outfit who persuaded them that a further prize, a bicycle for each of them, was waiting outside. As the prize giving event broke up no one noticed them following him out. They were driven to a house at the other end of the town and locked up."

"We have discovered that their father, James Kent, had received a threatening note at his office in London. It was not specific but indicated that action would be taken to 'make him pay'; you may well be aware of the extensive controversy involving the new cancer drug Demoniximol developed by Mr Kent's company. So the most logical thing is to assume that the children were taken for ransom to get at him. Investigations are ongoing and there is little I can say about that for the moment. What I suspect you are most interested in right now is that, while they had a horrible and scary experience, the children were not harmed and indeed they managed to escape. Without a doubt they are a very resourceful pair." He turns and smiles at the children as he says this and various cameras dotted around the group flash in unison. He continues: "Their escape also involves the two people on my left: Margaret, who works here at the library and Alice Carter, who is a reporter on the local weekly newspaper, the Maldon Express. I'll let them tell their own tale, Margaret, you first, right?"

Margaret stands up, goes to the microphone and begins to describe what happened. She says everyone at the library felt so bad about what occurred at the prize giving and that afterwards she promised to let me know if there were any developments. Then she describes how, a little later, I had found the box and instructions for one of the prizes - Jake's new smart watch – discovered the apparent location feature, and how we had then worked together to check it all out.

"Neither of us are that technical, but Alice came round and we looked at the instructions together. It appeared to have a tracker device on it. Alice do you want to take over at this point?" Well frankly I don't want to very much at all, I hate this sort of thing, but I go and take her place at the microphone. I have worked out what I think is a suitable starting point and go to the microphone holding my phone which is still recording.

"Right, the question everyone has been asking me is why we didn't just tell the police about the watch; not least that's what the Inspector here asked me." I turn and glance over my shoulder at Inspector Stuart as I try to get what comes next organised in my mind. "But as Margaret says, we weren't sure, we sort of worked it out as we went along and the instructions, appallingly badly translated from Japanese, didn't help much." A few people smiled or nodded at that; we've all been there. "As Margaret said, the watch appeared to have a tracking device on it, it's a children's model and this is, I guess, designed as a security feature. Anyway, we got it working or we thought we did, and it seemed to show the watch was not far away. So we drove towards what appeared to be the location to see if the gadget was doing what we thought it was. Once we were at what did prove to be the house, we thought we should physically check it out, just to be sure it was the place the tracker was identifying; we had little idea of how precisely it operated."

"The house appeared to have been left unguarded and we wondered, if we were right, if we could get the children out before anyone returned – assuming they were there that is. But there might have been someone there and if so it seemed logical to expect that they could be armed, so we went very carefully, first round one side of the house – where we found a flag that the kids had managed to hang out saying '**Help**', so that told us we were in the right place. A window was broken at the side of the house, so I opened it up, climbed in and had a look around. It appeared to be where the children had been held, but there was no sign of them and we assumed they had been moved. Then I went back out and we both went round to the other side of the house - where Jake and I collided at the corner. He came round on a bike and bowled me clean over; we now know they had got out just as we arrived, but hid in the garage when they heard the noise we made. They assumed it came from the kidnapper or an accomplice. At that stage we just reintroduced ourselves – the kids had met us here in the library at the prize giving – and we all went to my car aiming to get away from there as soon as we possibly could. The kids had already escaped but we were just glad to be there to see them safely on their way. We piled into my car, bikes and all – the kids wouldn't leave without them – and I drove them to the police station. The Inspector's right, Jake and Julie are a great pair of kids. That's it really. I'm just pleased they are safe and sound. We all are. Okay – over to Jake and Julie now I guess."

As I finish, pleasingly having got through it all without pushing my glasses up my nose even once, the Inspector comes up behind me to take over. He explains again that there is little he can say about the ongoing investigation, only that there are "various lines of enquiry" and that they "hope to make an arrest as soon as possible". What a clichéd message that is.

"This man, we know it's a man of course, committed a dreadful crime and we are determined to catch him." He says, then it's the turn of the children: the Inspector stresses to everyone that they are young, have been through a difficult time and that questions to them should be sensitive and will be limited. Then the microphone is lowered and put in front of and between them as they stand up to a barrage of further clicks and flashes as photos are taken, far more than for Margaret and me it must be said, but I suppose that's fair enough. The first question is predictable.

"I am quite sure that everyone's glad you are back at home safely and we all want to know how you escaped." I can't read her name badge from where I am sitting but I imagine the woman is from a national paper. The kids look at each other and Jake leans towards the microphone and starts to speak, hesitatingly at first, but he is soon caught up in the occasion and rattling along with his tale.

"Well, I suppose, well... it was the television... I mean we were watching a programme about cutting up sheets of paper to make things and it reminded me of a trick I had seen somewhere before. We kept trying the door, it was always locked, but then I looked through the keyhole and discovered that the kidnapper had left the key in the lock. We stuck a number of sheets of paper together and slid it under the door to catch the key when I pushed it out."

Julie interrupts.

"I helped, we did it together and it was my idea to take the bikes to get away. Anyway he'd said they were a present and I wanted to keep mine, my old one at home's gotten too small. Mum says we both grow as you watch." She grins as she says this and her last comment produces some chuckles.

There are more questions and they tell how, once out of the bedroom, they had waited and listened carefully to be sure there was no one in the house... how they had passed the time while they were locked up, for example playing Uno. And how, yes, they had been frightened, but "we knew people would be looking for us" and were determined to get out, so first they had made the flag – Julie's idea she says - and secondly, later on, Jake's key idea had worked. Their explaining that they never saw their abductor removes one line of possible questioning, one I am sure that the Inspector would have stamped on anyway.

"Tell us more about the room, were there other games?" One of the reporters follows up that point and Julie rattles on.

"There was a TV and lots of books and games, we both like Uno and play it at home. I won most games, but Jake didn't concentrate, he kept putting down the wrong colour." Again Julie raises a smile.

It has become clear that the extreme care that seemed to have been taken to ensure no harm came to the children was somewhat odd in the circumstances and as questions move into that area the Inspector resorts to "no comment" and promises to make further statements as the investigation continues. He also refuses to speculate about the reasons for the kidnapping and tells reporters that any questions about Mr Kent's company and the protests against it should be addressed to their press office; he gives out a telephone number and refuses to say more. Then he reminds everyone that in future the investigation is to be conducted by the CID from the police station in Chelmsford and that a contact sheet for that is available at the door.

He wraps the proceedings up.

"That's all for now, I must say a big thank to Margaret and Alice for what they did and a well done to Jake and Julie who appear to have coped so well with a scary situation and for all of them agreeing to be here today. Thank you all for coming and I would ask you to clear the library promptly now so that the staff can get it back to business as usual." At the end I think the occasion went pretty well and the Inspector kept off the question of any other much worse potential outcomes, mention of which might have upset the children. As the police move to take their leave he thanks us for being there and then leans towards me and speaks in a loud whisper.

"By the way the children told us they heard the sound of breaking glass, brings to mind the phrase 'breaking and entering' doesn't it?" I wonder whether to insist on it being an accident, but he is quickly gone. It seemed to be said very tongue in cheek; I hope so.

After a while only Margaret and I are left and the library is returning to business as usual.

"Well I'm glad that's over, I have to say that I'm much happier writing about things."

"Do you want a cuppa before you go back to your office? I think there are some biscuits in the back."

I award myself a break and accept Margaret's offer. Elizabeth Kent, who had refused to take any questions herself, has taken the kids back home and the police have left too, so it is just us for coffee.

"You said you hated speaking at things, but you did fine." I am grateful if someone thinks so, but I can't ever see it being on a par with writing.

"Thanks, that all seemed to go well and I'm glad it's over. I don't suppose there is anything we can add to the investigation so the police may not come back to us."

"Well only if we catch the guy, I suppose!" Yeah, right. The door opens and someone asks if Margaret is free, back to normal duties I guess. I tell her that I must get on too and that we will no doubt continue to talk about all this for a while yet.

Even now as I leave to go back to the office, a while after the press conference finished, there are still a couple of reporters waiting outside, they make a beeline for me, doubtless intent on asking more questions, but I don't stop.

"Sorry, guys, I have my own story to write up." I may not be on a national as they are, but I do have a lead story to write.

CHAPTER TWENTY SIX

A bit curious

It's mid-afternoon and I'm driving to Wickham Bishops because during the telephone call I made early on I successfully persuaded the Kents to give me an interview today. Elizabeth Kent hadn't been that keen, telling me that "surely that wretched press conference was enough"; I think it was telling her that if they saw me then after that they could refuse any further national media requests they got by just telling reporters to come to me that prompted her to agree. Of course some would persist but it's an approach which should genuinely make their lives a tad easier. We agreed a time for me to visit when I saw her at the library.

I pull into their drive, park and get out of the car. The house appears to be an expensively converted barn of some sort, my battered Mini looks very old and downmarket in such surroundings parked as it is next to the Kent's smart Volvo SUV. The Mini is the car I learnt to drive in, and had been in the family as a second runabout for years and years before my dad let me have it when I went to university and he bought Mum something newer. I've been told that it's a classic and that if it was properly done up it would be worth a few bob. Hmmm, maybe. I ring the bell and Elizabeth Kent opens the door, she really does look like a different person from the one the kids were delivered back to now the strain of what happened is in the past. She looked better at the press conference, but here at home she is clearly putting the worry behind her. She leads me through a spacious hall into a lovely modern, yet country style, kitchen. It seems to gleam and shout out about how much it cost; I reckon I could buy a small flat for the amount of money that was probably involved. She offers me a drink, I ask for tea and she puts the kettle on. We chatter about the press conference until it's boiled and drinks can be made. There's no sign of James Kent, which I have to say does not surprise me; I don't know of course, but I wonder if he is in London.

"We are so *very* grateful for all you did," she says, sitting down and giving me a beaming smile, "to you and the girl from the library, I dread to think what might have happened if you hadn't found them. Sorry, what's your friend's name?"

"Margaret." Elizabeth, she tells me to call her that, continues to smile and, before I can join her sitting down the kids rush into the kitchen amid an avalanche of chatter and giggling. Faced with me they turn shy for a moment, Jake just says: "Hello" and then Julie finds her voice.

"You saved us, can I hug you?" She asks and I stoop down and we do just that. A mug of tea is in front of me as I now sit down at the breakfast bar and I offer Elizabeth a thank you for the drink. I realise I am starving, lunchtime was kind of busy, I plead extreme hunger and a large tin of biscuits appears on the worktop, delivered by Julie. It's shortbread in a tin decorated with a Christmas design.

"Well, you two seem none the worse for your ordeal, though I am sure it was scary, are you both okay now?" Nods and giggles suggest they are and I verify the fact with Elizabeth.

"Can I ask you some questions?" They both nod and scramble up onto kitchen stools alongside us. Jake's "Can I have a..." is cut off by a look from Elizabeth. Visible biscuits equal feeling hunger automatically at that age as I remember. I put the lid back on the tin to minimise temptation and it is quickly forgotten.

"One thing first," I reach for the bag I have hung over the back of the stool, "this is yours Jake, it was left in the library and Margaret asked me to get it back to you. There are the instructions to that smart watch of yours inside, you may want to have a look at that." Jake thanks me and, having whispered to him that I did not eat his chocolate, I proceed with my questions.

What takes place next is not the kind of interview any of my training has prepared me for and I am glad I switched on the recorder on my phone before I began to ask them to tell me about their experiences. Because it all comes out at once, first from Jake, but with Julie leaving little time before chipping in and saying as much as he does. Mostly it seems they are both talking at once and talking apace. Once when Jake tries to stop her, Julie responds with "don't talk when I'm interrupting". They giggle in a way that suggests it's a well-used remark and I wonder if it is one I would dare use with Smaug, hmmm, perhaps not. They really do seem to be fine.

I try to take notes of the key points as the recording may well prove somewhat less than straightforward to decipher. It's clear what happened in the library, they thought Farther Christmas and the bikes were part of the formal proceedings, something I find myself admitting was a pretty good plan on the part of their abductor and all too easy for them to have been taken in by the deception. As their tale goes on it becomes clear that though they had a very scary time, there were no actual threats to life or limb, it was the uncertainty that got to them. Unsurprisingly so. But they saw little or nothing of whoever took them and the rest of what went on seems to get stranger and stranger. He not only did not hurt them, he seems to have gone out of his way to minimise their discomfort. The room was comfortable, warm, it had a television, books, games and they were given a regular supply of food and drink. Somehow I feel it seems to indicate more than being just a way to keep them quiet, it seems to indicate a genuine concern for them. Not at all like one's image of a ruthless kidnapper. Whatever the reason it made their ordeal a little easier, though, of course, at the time no one – least of all the children - was to know that the threat was not far worse, though I suppose no one knows how matters would have played out if they had not got away.

"One thing I didn't know until the press conference was how you in fact managed to escape. How did you think of that? It was very clever of you." Jake beams with pride and gives me a full description of his idea again: the trick had come back to him as they watched a television presenter doing handicrafts of some sort, but he still can't remember where he had first heard of it. Probably at school. Anyway it worked. Clever. I have vague memories of knowing the trick as a child too. Julie interrupts, wanting her turn.

"I helped too, the gap under the door wasn't big enough and I squished the carpet down to help get the key into the room."

"When he delivered breakfast, Julie screamed and threatened to burst out, I think he went downstairs too quickly after that and forgot to take the key." They seem a very sensible pair, and such an experience could have been so much worse and their imprisonment much longer. I thank them all and go to take my leave. Just then the doorbell rings. Elizabeth goes and opens up. It's a police constable with the two bicycles, evidently their return has been approved and the Inspector has been as good as his word sending a message that he "moved heaven and Earth to get them back quickly". The children greet them with delight and wheel them into the hall.

"Leave them for the moment," says Elizabeth and I take a moment with her while the kids are busy stowing the bikes somewhere at the back of the hall.

"It must be such a relief that they were not harmed." I say to Elizabeth who is holding the door for me.

"Yes, they seem to have been in no danger, indeed they seem fine and it is apparently no problem having the bikes around. They insisted on having them. It's a curious business and you know what – I probably shouldn't tell you this – but it looks like he never intended to harm the children and was always going to let them go. The police found a key to the bedroom taped to the back of the wardrobe. It seems likely that was because he must have been going to tell them how to get out at some stage."

"Well, that certainly is a bit curious, as you say." And puzzling too. "But I wonder when they would have been freed? There was never any ransom demand as I understand it."

"No, none, the whole thing's all very weird, just that initial vague threat James got at the office about being 'made to pay'. But maybe his plans were just overtaken by events, by them getting out and what you and Margaret did to get them safely away. Maybe he had just not got to the moment for sending the ransom demand."

"Well, it would be nice to think so. Anyway I will be following the story, you know, about what the police do now and such like, so do let me know if anything else happens, anything at all." I give her my card and they all gather at the front door as I start to go out. As I walk towards my car, the kids are still clustering alongside her at the door and they wave and shout goodbyes before the door closes. Before I can get into my car another vehicle enters the driveway and draws up beside me. James Kent gets out of a smart Audi SUV, maybe this is what he calls a runabout to get him to the station in the morning; how the other half live. He comes over to me, calling out.

"Alice, I'm so glad I caught you." He doesn't explain where he's been. "I want to thank you, you and Margaret, this could all have been so much worse. We owe you a great deal. Maybe you have a great career ahead of you as an investigative reporter." Very magnanimous, and he remembers our names. I hope he's right about the career.

"Well, I'm pleased we could help and it all worked out alright. The children seem fine, that's the main thing, though it must have been very scary for them. I hope they don't get nightmares. Don't you think it's all a bit odd though?"

"What do you mean?"

"They don't seem to have been in real danger, I hear that the police think he had arranged to release them and I saw the room they were kept in, it had been carefully equipped to make them comfortable, well as comfortable as possible under the circumstances. All rather curious, he's not your typical kidnapper, that's for sure. And taking them must have been done for a reason, maybe the kids got out before any ransom note could be delivered. I suppose such a note might have asked for money... or perhaps action to make that drug of yours more widely available. Or maybe both. What do you think?" James Kent cannot be feeling at his best, well would anyone be in such circumstances? It's more than that though: his face looks sufficiently wary that I wonder if I have struck a nerve.

"Much more likely that there was a money demand to come, I think." He says, speaking in a measured tone. I wonder some more. If it was done because of the drug then it might explain the care taken with the children, whoever did it wanted action and not to cause harm to the kids.

"I'm not sure I agree." He really is looking sheepish now and I wonder a bit more as a thought strikes me and I put my wondering into words.

"Wait a minute... did you get a ransom note?" I pause as the thought grows in my mind and he looks more and more uncomfortable. "In fact did you *pay* a ransom? My God, I think you did!" Kent's discomfort grows visibly as I say this, his response is instant and there is now an angry edge to his voice and he holds himself stiffly.

"Certainly not, maybe a demand would have come later, we were just lucky the children got out when they did. Anyway thanks again, I must get on, I promised to spend time with the family today."

"But don't you think..." He doesn't let me continue.

"I really must go in and see the children, I'm sorry." He turns and heads towards the front door reaching and getting a key from his pocket as he does so.

Frankly I don't find his denial credible, he walks on and I watch him reach the front door and let himself in. His demeanour very much makes me feel I struck a nerve and I wonder some more.

In fact I go on wondering all the way back to Maldon.

CHAPTER TWENTY SEVEN
He deserved a beer

He had taken the money to his own house after the successful pickup in Chelmsford and stored it away in the wardrobe in his bedroom. He found himself giving a wry smile as he pushed the packages to the back of the cupboard and pulled an old dressing gown over the top to hide them from view, though of course the money would surely be found fast enough if there was a search. However, he was confident that he had covered his tracks too well for that to be a danger, and anyway he did not intend that the money would remain in his house for very long.

Now he just had to deal with the matter of the children.

He went outside again, got back in the car and drove back to the rented house, driving up the drive and round the corner to stop in front of the garage. Even before he had got out of the car he could see to his surprise and horror that the back door was standing a little ajar. What on Earth? He got out so fast that the sleeve of his jacket got caught on the car door and stopped him for a second, shaking himself free he strode to the back door and looked in. The kitchen was empty and, as he listened, the whole house seemed silent. He paused long enough to pull on his gloves and hastened through to the hall and looked up the stairs. The angle of sight meant that it was not clear whether the door to the bedroom was standing open or closed, he rushed up the stairs two at a time and by the time he was half way up he could see clearly: the door was standing a little open. He went up the final few steps and gave it a slight push.

The room was empty.

The door to the small bathroom stood open too, the children were gone and so too were both the bicycles. They must have taken them and used them to get away. A large sheet of paper was on the floor across the doorway, looking at it he realised almost at once what they must have done, and he slipped his hand around the door and felt the key in the inside lock to confirm it. It was an old trick he remembered from his own childhood. He cursed under his breath, he must have left the room too hastily when he left to pick up the ransom and inadvertently left the key in the lock. He cursed out loud, he thought he had overlooked nothing.

His immediate thought now was that he had to get out of the house. Right now. He didn't know how long the kids had been gone and he wondered where they would go, surely they wouldn't cycle all the way home to Wickham Bishops, he thought, though that would mean he had more time. Maybe they would head for the police station in the town or even go back to the library. Whatever destination they chose he had no doubt that once they reached it the police could then be arriving at the house very soon afterwards. In fact they could, he realised, arrive at any moment. There was nothing in the house to incriminate him other perhaps than the Father Christmas outfit and he would take that with him. There might be fingerprints in the house, of course, though he had always worn white gloves with the red and white suit and had wiped down all the things he had bought and arranged in the room he had set aside for the children before his plan commenced. He had gloves on now. However, even if his prints were checked he had no criminal record and they would not be able to help to track him down. He descended the stairs at speed, shut the back door behind him, backed the car up so that it was turned back to face the road and then drove slowly and carefully home in a manner designed not to draw any attention to himself. Once there he left the engine running while he opened the garage doors, then drove the car inside. Since putting up the metal screens in the rental house he was now the proud owner of an electric screwdriver, using this it took only a few minutes for him to change the number plates back to his own. He got the red and white suit out of the car and took it round to the back of the house and down the garden to where an incinerator stood already largely primed with rubbish and garden refuse. He pushed the suit into the top, added the white gloves, struck a match to set it alight and left it to burn. Everything there was dry and the flames took hold fast. Then he wrapped the stolen number plates tightly in a cut down black plastic bin liner, added a few stones, and set off again in the car, this time going a little way out of Maldon itself towards Heybridge. He parked in the car park at Heybridge Basin, an area adjacent to where the canal runs along its final stretch to join the river Blackwater. It is a popular spot in the summer for both walkers, fisher-folk and the sailing and boating fraternity and formed the very last part of a waterway that stretched for very many miles. Its popularity was heightened by its having a free car park, something of which he very much approved.

It was again a cold day and there were only two other cars in the car park, most likely dog walkers he thought, everyone else who might be there no doubt had Christmas to prepare for. He reckoned there should be few people about. He tucked the package containing the number plates lengthwise under his arm so that it was hardly visible and climbed up the half dozen steps to the canal towpath. He turned right along the canal and away from the busy area at the end of the path in the other direction where there were two pubs, and a tea room run by the famous Wilkins jam company who were headquartered in nearby Tiptree, and walked a few hundred yards along to a point where there were no more boats moored against the canal bank. Then he stopped and stood looking round him and listening. He could neither see nor hear anyone. He knelt down as if tying a shoelace and slid the package containing the number plates below the surface, where it rapidly sank and disappeared out of sight into the murky water.

He walked back towards the car at a leisurely pace, passing ducks and a swan swimming serenely on the canal alongside him, then, at the point where boats were moored along the banks, he continued on past the car park and along the last couple of hundred yards to The Old Ship pub. The walks along the canal and river path and the location on the estuary made this whole area a popular spot and this was a pub he had visited many times over the years.

Having reached this stage of his plan, and seemingly survived the escape of the children, he reckoned he deserved a drink. He bought a beer and ordered an all-day breakfast at the bar. The main lunch time rush was now past and the pub was not crowded, he sat by the window from where he could see out across the river. Almost at once someone came and sat in the booth next door to him. They vaguely recognised each other, though only from crossing paths in the pub on previous visits.

"Hello there, what are you up to today?" The question and the act of having to engage with someone so soon after what he had been doing gave him a shock and for a moment he was not sure what to say. Gathering his wits, it was no risk after all, he replied, turning the conversation to the current festive time of year.

"Just avoiding Christmas shopping for a bit longer, I guess." They chatted a little about the coming holiday, then his food arrived and the other man was joined by a couple he clearly knew well and he turned away. He realised that, while he had kept his cool throughout all he had done so far, now it was almost over he had become quite agitated at that moment, it was probably finding the children gone, rather than all the other activities he had been engaging in that did it. He took a deep breath, heaved a long, silent sigh and turned his attention to his food.

During the time he then took to drink his pint and eat his all-day breakfast he could think of nothing from the past few days that might act to give him away. All anyone who had seen him at the library would remember was the Father Christmas suit with a big white beard obscuring the wearer's face. His car was not new, special or memorable, the number plates displayed on it were not his own for the duration of the plan, and now lying at the bottom of the canal they should not come to light for a long time, if ever. The children were, he imagined, now back home safe and sound. He had never meant them any harm, indeed he had equipped the room to make them as comfortable as possible in the circumstances; in fact their imprisonment had always been the bit of his plan he liked least. He had even left an envelope with money in it under the windscreen wiper of the car from which he had taken the number plates, and had done so after checking to see what new ones would cost. There was only one person he had wanted to hurt, and if possible to prompt action from, and that was James Kent.

He reckoned the man had most certainly had a fright and it had cost him too, as well as the money he had been forced to pay out, the first reports of the kidnapping would doubtless link his being targeted to his refusal to supply the drug Demoniximol to the NHS at a reasonable rate. He felt that there was a good chance that the continuing publicity would see him changing his mind and acting so that the drug eventually become more generally available. Indeed he had done his best to make that so. All in all he was within reach of a good result he thought. He continued to muse on this as, his meal finished, he left the pub and walked back along the canal to his car.

When he got back home he got out the bags of cash from the wardrobe and went through them with exaggerated care. Apparently Kent had decided to trust that he meant what he said about freeing the children; as predicted he seemed to have gone for a quick fix given all that was going on in his company. As he searched through the packages he could find nothing designed to trap him, nothing jumped out and sprayed the money or himself with fluorescent paint, nothing appeared to be radioing his whereabouts to the authorities. The money seemed to be completely clean, though as requested all the notes were used. He was pretty sure it was all just as it had been packed by the bank. He repacked the cash in manageable bundles and stowed it away in the two bags he had ready for what would come next.

He would leave it for a few days, then there was just one more important thing that needed to be done.

CHAPTER TWENTY EIGHT
We need to check

Some days after the children were returned safely to their home the situation at Maldon police station had largely returned to its normal mode of operations. The ongoing investigation was now being coordinated and worked on by CID officers from the larger police station in Chelmsford. The small team in Maldon, drawn in by the location and urgency, were again able to concern themselves primarily with local matters though, given that the children had been imprisoned in a house in the town, all officers were charged with keeping a keen eye on developments.

"I reckon that's the end of it, the kidnapper is long gone, he might have been from anywhere in the country, it was only that James Kent lives here that makes for a local link." One of the police constables addressed his remark to Sergeant Jane after their usual morning team briefing, a briefing that currently daily continued to mention the need to look out for anything suspicious that might link to the kidnapping, though without much specific guidance as to what might actually be considered suspicious being possible.

"I am sure the CID are doing their best, the investigation is continuing and I would hate to think anyone would get away with abducting kids like that. Maybe there will be a breakthrough. If so I hope it's us that gets it. Meantime we must all keep it in mind. You never know." To some extent Jane was toeing the party line on the matter, but privately it seemed to her that the man had covered his tracks all too well and was now in the wind. She also knew that the case would not rate the same priority now that the children had been found and were safely back at home; this might be regrettable, but given current police resourcing it was just how things were now. More would be being done if a ransom had been involved, but it looked as if the children's escape had happened before a ransom demand could be issued. Even so various investigations had occurred, for instance, local bed and breakfasts, hotels and so on had been checked in case it was someone visiting the location who had been the perpetrator, but no likely suspects had been discovered. Indeed, as her constable had said, the kidnapper could be anywhere and if he had been visiting the district then surely he would have stayed in the house in which the children were held. After all virtually nothing about him was known. A man, yes, maybe average height, maybe forty or so years upwards, but the Christmas outfit had kept his face and physique a complete mystery. She had discussed the crime with husband Philip the previous evening and they were pretty much of one mind about it. Neither felt it was at all likely that anyone would be found.

"I am just glad it's all over," he had said, "it was a dreadful thing to happen on my patch, as it were, but the library's back to normal now and I for one would be happy never to hear about the matter ever again, though I suppose it's not nice to think of whoever it was still being free. I doubt he's a threat now though, it looked like the whole thing was only done to get at James Kent – it was a protest - so I reckon there's no likelihood of a repeat." They let the matter lie and had found themselves broadly in agreement.

After the morning briefing Jane went back to her desk to find a message relating to the crime, an email from Inspector Stuart in Chelmsford. It explained that, amongst the many hundreds of messages sent to James Kent about the drug, two of the letter writers had an address in or near Maldon. Because they were close to the house concerned, she was asked to visit them and "check them out", although the Inspector's message conceded that "it does seem a very long shot". She acknowledged the note and printed out the addresses that needed a visit. With no more pressing matters it could be done at once.

She let Constable Brown drive and they headed for the first address: an H. J. Case living in the nearby village of Goldhanger, a small hamlet three or four miles outside the town consisting of a few houses, two pubs and a church. Once there, they turned right at the Chequers pub and drove down Fish Lane. Leaving the constable in the car outside she approached a row of small terraced cottages, spotted the right number and went to the door, glancing over her shoulder at the car to make sure she was still within sight as she knocked using the large wrought iron ring that acted to summon attention. After a brief pause an elderly woman, wearing an apron and wiping her hands with a cloth, opened the door and, seeing the uniform, immediately adopted a shocked expression. She spoke with a gasp.

"The police, oh my goodness, is it bad news?" She put her hand, and the cloth, to her mouth. The Sergeant found that this was a common reaction to seeing an unexpected policeman on your doorstep, and sometimes, of course, she was the bearer of bad news. One of her least favourite tasks was bringing news of accidents to people. It was one of the things most, if not all, police officers did not look forward to doing. This was especially true if the news was to notify someone of a death, and these particularly grim assignments were sometimes referred to as a death knock. Sergeant Jane had become regarded as being good at such tasks, and so she was, but nevertheless she sometimes thought that this just brought her rather more than her fair share of such tasks.

So, well understanding the woman's feelings, she responded at once aiming to reassure her.

"No, no, it's nothing bad, nothing to worry about, just a question or two. Are you H. J. Case?"

"Helen Case, yes, that's me." She resumed her hand wiping. "Sorry, you caught me baking." The smell wafting through the house seemed to confirm the fact as did a small deposit of flour that touching her face with the cloth had deposited on her cheek.

"I'm sorry, I hope nothing will spoil. Do you live here alone?"

"I do yes, my husband died some years back."

"I'm sorry. Just a quick question for you. A while ago did you write a letter to the company Demonaxx about their cancer drug and the controversy over its cost?"

"It's several weeks ago, but yes I did, my sister Brenda, she lives down in Sussex, well she used to, she died a few months back. The doctors reckoned that new drug would have helped, but she couldn't get it. I think it's a disgrace, holding the NHS to ransom and allowing people to die like that, it's a crime, it's pitting profit against peoples' lives." She paused for a second then rather than continuing what sounded as if it could be a long full on rant, she changed tack and asked: "What's this all about? Surely I'm not in trouble, I think my letter was actually rather polite in the circumstances."

"No, of course you're not in trouble, and I'm sorry about your sister. You had a perfect right to send a letter. Now did you read about the children being kidnapped in Maldon a few days ago?"

"Yes, I did, terrible business, but those kids got away though didn't they, what's that to do with..." Jane interrupted, seeing that this was beginning to take too long.

"Well, the CEO of the company is James Kent, it was his children that were taken and one line of inquiry is that the crime was linked to the protests about the drug, we are contacting people who wrote to the company, well the ones living in or near Maldon."

"I was angry about it, that's true, but do I look like a kidnapper? I read in the newspapers that it was a man, a man in a Father Christmas outfit." She spreads her arms in a "who me?" sort of gesture and the cloth she was holding wafts flour into the air prompting an exclamation of "Oops!"

"I'm quite sure it wasn't you, Mrs Case, but thanks for sparing me a moment, I am very sorry to interrupt your baking, but I'm sure you will understand that we need to check every possibility. Goodbye to you and have a nice Christmas."

"Okay, yes of course, sorry I can't help. I hope you catch whoever it was." As Mrs Case closed the door and went back to her kitchen, Sergeant Jane returned to the car and they made ready to set off and check out the second address.

"No joy there," she said to her companion. "An elderly lady living alone. Her sister could have done with the drug evidently, that's why she wrote. One down, one to go." Constable Brown pulled away from the kerb as she spoke and headed the car towards the second address.

CHAPTER TWENTY NINE
Sorry to bother you

As Sergeant Jane was leaving Goldhanger he sat at his kitchen breakfast bar having a late breakfast and reading a spread out copy of *The Daily Telegraph* as he finished his second piece of toast. Over the last day or two he had found only one brief mention of his crime in its pages, and today there was nothing, a fact that made him think that the hunt for him was being scaled right down or running into the ground for want of any lead; hopefully both he thought. With the children safely back at home and Kent evidently saying nothing about a ransom having been paid he felt safe. He put the newspaper aside, made himself a second cup of tea and reviewed the situation in his mind again to be sure that he had overlooked nothing. He felt his plan had gone well. He felt he was in the clear. The time of year had helped he felt, after all who paid any attention to a Father Christmas in December? He had been able to adopt a disguise that did not even seem to be a disguise. And of course the children having won the competition was a great stroke of luck that put them in the perfect place from which he had been able not only to take them, but also to accomplish doing so with no noise or fuss until they were actually locked in the bedroom.

He went through the sequence of events in his mind. His preparations had been low risk and done with care. On the day he had only been in the library for a few minutes and he could see no problem there; no one had taken any notice of him, all eyes had been looking ahead, and anyway he had been unrecognisable. He was sure the drive that took the children to the rented house had been unobserved and, of course, the stolen number plates had been fitted to his car removing another potential problem. He had faced away from the children as he drove as they sat in the back of the car, indeed he had led the way out of the library and led the way too when they had gone into the house and up the stairs; so in fact they had hardly seen him at all. They had heard his voice of course, though not for very long, but he had no distinctive accent so that should not be a problem and besides it was unlikely that they would ever hear him speak again. Even the picking up of the money in the street in Chelmsford appeared to have gone without a hitch. He would know by now if Kent had been successful in having him followed, and if an attempt had been made to follow then his tactics with the ticket machine must have worked. He had no way of knowing which it was. He had seen in the mirror that he had caused a jam at the car park exit and having thus held cars up behind him, he was therefore as sure as he could be that he had not been followed.

The children escaping had certainly been an unexpected development. He had very much not planned for that. He had read in the paper a description of how they had done it and it was just as he supposed; he had to admit to one slip, leaving the key in the lock when he had rushed downstairs with the tray because the girl Julie screaming earlier had unnerved him a little. On the other hand he had always intended them no harm, indeed he regretted the necessity of what he had done to them, but had been able to think of no effective alternative plan. He was always intending to let them go in due course. He had been lucky, their escape could have come at a worse moment; much earlier and it might have seen the whole plan be stillborn. There was only one more thing to do now and he did not regard that as posing any sort of risk.

He was jolted out of his musing by a ring at the front door. He wasn't expecting anyone. He went through to the hall and opened the door to find himself faced with a policeman, well a policewoman, a uniformed Sergeant. For a second or two he was speechless, his heart went to his mouth, finally he stuttered one word: Yes?" Then he rapidly pulled himself together.

"Sorry to bother you, Sir, I wonder if I could ask you a couple of questions." Seeing that imminent arrest did not seem to be the order of the day he regained his poise, someone like himself would be expected to be cooperative, he was sure, so he resolved to be just that. He gave her a smile.

"Of course, Sergeant, do you want to come in? I was just finishing a late breakfast and there's tea on the go if you would like." Sergeant Jane found she was about ready for a cup of something, she decided to leave her driver colleague in the car, gave him a wave to indicate she was going in, took off her hat and went inside as the man held the front door open for her.

"Yes, thank you, oh... you are Gerald Davies, right?"

"I am indeed. Gerry, if you like." He led the way through to a smart kitchen and offered her a seat on one of four stools ranged along a central worktop bar. She sat down.

"Tea, yes? Now what's this all about? How can I help? I hope I haven't forgotten to pay a parking fine somewhere." She nodded to the tea and explained as he poured some for her from a pot already in place on the worktop.

"Milk, but no sugar please. Now I am told that you wrote a letter to the pharmaceutical company Demonaxx about their new cancer drug. Is that right?"

"I did indeed. I considered joining that protest group, CV something or other, but in the end I just wrote a personal protest at what they were doing. My wife died of cancer some months ago and, although I suppose you can never know a hundred percent, it seems that if she could have got that drug it might well have given her a little longer to live. I hope that's no problem. It was weeks ago." He had resisted joining the protest group specifically so that its lists did not include his name, but his message had been written right at the beginning of the protests and certainly before the formal protest group had been set up. He had forgotten all about his letter and had created his plan only later on when the ongoing protests seemed to be achieving nothing. It was, he admitted to himself, something else to which he had not given sufficient thought.

"No, Sir, no problem. I understand, and I'm sorry about your wife."

"If I may, if it's no problem, why do you ask?" Sergeant Jane sipped her tea and explained.

"Did you see the news about the recent child kidnapping here in Maldon?" He nodded, not trusting himself to speak for a second.

"Well, one line of enquiry is that it was carried out by someone with a grudge against Mr Kent's company – it was his children that were abducted. A couple of the many hundreds of letters and emails sent to the company were from addresses here in the town so we are just checking, I hope you understand."

"Yes, I'm sure you have to be very thorough. I did read about it and, yes, suppose that I certainly do have a grudge against those money grabbing people, I think they are behaving despicably - that's why I sent the letter, but I hope I don't look like the ruthless gangster type, it was just one letter. I wanted to help swell the number of protests, make sure that they got a great many... that they noticed what so many people were thinking. Every little helps. Isn't that what they say? Maybe all the protests will make them think again." She took in the man sitting in front of her, he looked like a retired accountant, dressed neatly in a sports jacket and tie just to have a solitary breakfast. Seemingly only another sad grieving protester, she assumed that, whilst some who sent messages were opportunistic trouble makers, most had sound and positive motives.

"No, Sir, you don't, but perhaps I should ask you where you were on the morning of the abduction." She quoted him the date on which the children had been abducted.

"I am not entirely sure, now I'm retired and living on my own since I lost my wife, one day is much like another. I usually go for a walk each morning, I think that day I drove to Goldhanger, if you go past the church you can walk across the fields and back along the river. I have no idea if I saw anyone that day, it's not usually busy out there, but I walk there regularly and then sometimes have a sandwich or something at the Chequers - you know the village pub – afterwards. There are often people I know and can chat to in there, I could check, I suppose."

"I know the spot you mean." It was a place she and Philip used to go and walk when they first met – and indeed it remained a favourite spot. She knew it well and her last visit to Helen Case had been nearby. It was a location that always prompted good memories for her. They chatted about the location for a minute or two while she finished her tea. She concluded Gerald Davies was harmless.

"I don't think anything else will be necessary, I mustn't keep you, and thanks for your help, something else I can cross off my list. Now I must get on. Thank you for my tea." She wished him a merry Christmas as she walked back through the hall and they said goodbyes at the door. She returned to the car and got in.

"I bet whoever that was gave you a cuppa." She smiled. The constable was right.

"Yes, as a matter of fact he did. A nice man: someone else writing to the company because he had lost a relative with cancer – his wife in his case – someone else who might have been helped had that drug been available. The way these things work is an utter mystery to me. Let's get back to the station. I hope they are having more luck with this over in Chelmsford."

Back in the house Gerald Davies heaved a huge sigh of relief. He had no alibi for the morning in question and could only hope that the idea of the pub and people he knew to some extent, which was in fact true, would be sufficient for no further checking to be done. Certainly the Sergeant had seemed satisfied. So now that experience was over, if anything he felt even safer than before, and he did not feel he had given out any wrong signals. If the only thing that had brought the police to his door was his being one of many hundreds of messages sent protesting about the drug pricing issue, then he reckoned he was okay – a tree hidden in a forest as it were. He had no regrets, well he regretted giving the children a frightening time, but he kept telling himself that it had been the only way he could think of to achieve the outturn he wanted.

One his aims was to prompt Kent to rethink the question of making the drug readily available. He wondered what impact his latest note might have had. It said only: *The children was phase 1 – make the drug available or it gets serious.* He wished he could be a fly on the wall of the man's no doubt plush office, then maybe he would be able to judge if a change of heart was likely or not.

Then, belatedly, he remembered that there had been £100,000 in cash hidden in the wardrobe just above the policewoman's head as she drank her tea. The thought made him chuckle out loud. He had burnt the sacks he had used to collect the money, but he thought he had better do something about the cash sooner rather than later to get matters finished. It was too late to do anything today, he had planned the final step as a job best done first thing in the morning.

CHAPTER THIRTY

This is going to be great

I am driving home, that is I am going to my family home. The distance from Maldon is not so far, but it is a more difficult journey than the number of miles might suggest; not least because of the sheer unpredictability of the Dartford Crossing, the tunnel and bridge route over the River Thames. Everybody hates the crossing: traffic apart that's because you have to pay - sit a jam for half an hour: that will be £2.50 if you please. It's Saturday and I am making the journey to collect various possessions ahead of my moving into Margaret's flat later in the day. What I am collecting is mostly clothes and books, though there is one piece of furniture: a small pine table that has been in my bedroom for years and acts as a desk. I think it's a good idea to have a place to sit at quietly in my own room, though I am sure we are going to get on fine. I know "my flat" will be shared, but I'm excited about it and I'm thinking of it as my first real independent home, after all for most of my time at university I was in a jam-packed house with seven other students. It was somewhere to live at reasonable cost, it was fun, but, though the dictionary defines home rather blandly just as "somewhere to live" it was not really deserving of the word home in the fullest sense of how the word is used. I am so overdue to move out of my current cramped room; it's so small that if I ever became pregnant I don't think I would be able to get inside.

I pull into the drive and go into the house. It's the first time I have visited since the kidnapping incident so I get an extra-long hug from my mother who gushes about what she sees as my lucky survival.

"It's just *so* nice to see you and I am so glad you are safe and sound, what a terrible incident, you might have been captured or, or... well, worse." She does not utter the word kidnap, we both know exactly what she is referring to as the "incident". I try to play it down.

"It's a while back now Mum and it all ended well. I'm fine, absolutely fine and looking forward to this flat move. My job is on the up and up since the incident, as you call it, and now I have a proper place to live. You must come and see, wait until after the holiday period, then, if we pick a good day we can do a trip on the river or something."

"Yes, that would be nice, Maldon's a nice town and I am glad the jobs good – as long as it is not going to regularly put you in such danger. Give me another hug." We hug again, me thinking that I will be back very soon for Christmas day and we will probably have this all over again. Never mind, I'm lucky to have parents who care – and a mother who cooks so well! I change the subject by asking about lunch. I am pretty sure it will be a roast and I quickly find that I'm right.

"Roast lamb today and then turkey on Christmas Day, but you know that we always have turkey - it's a family tradition." Right, like not opening any presents until after lunch and then sleeping through the Queen's speech because we are all so full; replete is the right word, I think, which has amidst how the dictionary defines it the worded stuffed.

My father appears from what is virtually a cupboard but which is always referred to as his study and we go through much the same ground, though he is less adamant and moves on more quickly. I update them about the job, the slight change that seems to be occurring in my work and my hopes about it for the future. Then I have time to do a bit of sorting in my old bedroom before lunch. I take the table I plan to use as a make shift desk downstairs and discover it fits in the car after a bit of a struggle and with about a hair's breadth to spare on either side. That stored safely I will arrange the other stuff around it; I find a selection of bags and black sacks laid out ready in my room, my mother has anticipated my disorganisation and frankly that will help. There are also a number of cardboard boxes, which will be useful for books. I am beginning to pack up clothes, toiletries and various other detritus and consider whether I do really need to take three hairdryers when I have one in Maldon already, when I get the call for lunch.

A home cooked meal is a great treat and we chatter aimlessly about family matters.

"I must tell you what happened at school the other day..." At one point my mother launches into a long story about kids in the reception class she teaches at the local primary school. Evidently at one point three children were playing a great game involving a conversation with a stuffed animal. As the game progressed and as the scenario got quite serious, one child held the animal up and said pointedly to the youngest in the group "You *do know* it's not real don't you?"

"It can be hard work, but there is always something to make you smile." There are occasions when any mention of children, so easy to make when you are a teacher, seems to lead on to questions about boyfriends and settling down. I am far too young, and anyway I would need a decent boyfriend first, but evidently I am already more than old enough for her to dream of grandchildren. Maybe its's my imagination, anyway today there is nothing of this sort, maybe she has enough to think about regarding my recent exploits.

I help with the washing up and then my father helps me pack the car, finally it's time for the return trip. We say our goodbyes and note that the next time we are all together it will be Christmas, damn it, make a mental note, I still have to get them presents.

*

I send Margaret a text saying roughly what time I would get back, I need her to be there as I don't have a key yet. She replies saying that a key awaits me and so too does a welcome drink. I plan to go straight there and unload the car, then pick up my other stuff from the cubby hole I am now leaving. My landlady was very nice about my departure and we are parting on good terms.

I ring the bell and Margaret opens the door waving a set of shiny new keys.

"Welcome, this is going to be great."

"Did you have to get those cut, I should pay you for them."

"No problem, these are what your predecessor left behind, let me give you a hand." We go to and fro up and down the stairs to get all my stuff inside. At one point a whole box collapses spilling a load of books down the stairs and making sufficient noise for the tenant of the downstairs flat to stick their head out to see what is going on. I apologise, and between us Margaret and I collect them up, she is totally unfazed by my messy moving in and I take that as good sign for our future share.

"Do you want me to come with you up the road to get the rest?"

"No need, and anyway I think I will have to put stuff on the front seat to make it possible in one trip." I disappear to complete my move and by the evening, after another session of up and down the stairs, we settle down to enjoy a snack together (Margaret had lunch at her parents too) and a glass or two of wine. I fall into bed surrounded by boxes and bags; the sorting out and storing away will be done tomorrow.

With my job and living arrangements having taken a turn for the better I reckon I can put the kidnap incident, my mother's words, behind me and get into my new routine of life.

CHAPTER THIRTY ONE

Fame at last

A week or so later

I phone Elizabeth Kent, I do not regard doing so as work and I have nothing specific to ask her about the crime. This is more for my own piece of mind.

"Hello, Elizabeth, it's Alice Carter from the Maldon Express. I wonder if I could have a quick word." My initial reception is a touch frosty, I know the family were hounded by the press for a while after the event, despite my advice about fending off such enquiries.

"Oh... what is it?"

"Don't worry, I am not phoning with my press hat on, forgive me - I just wanted a private word. I can't help worrying being involved as I was, and now a little time has passed I just wanted to know – are Jake and Julie alright, no lingering effects?"

"Right, well it's kind of you to ask. And I'm pleased to say that they do seem to be doing fine. They don't have nightmares, they seem happy with the bicycles and they mention the whole business less now, especially with Christmas so nearly upon us they do have plenty else to think about. Though we would all love to know what it was all about and who the perpetrator was. There appears to be no sign of the police getting anywhere in terms of finding that out. Unless... have you heard anything?"

"No, nothing. I am inclined to think we won't now. He's long gone and I reckon the police won't prioritise it now that the kids are safe. Anyway I am pleased to hear you say that they are fine. They are great kids, say hello for me. Sorry to bother you, but I really couldn't stop thinking about them."

"That's okay, thanks... and have a happy Christmas. Goodbye." I say goodbye, add Christmas wishes and put the phone down, pleased that she is able to report good news.

The police investigatory activity regarding the kidnapping seems to have slowed right down now; not so much dead slow as stop. As I said to Elizabeth on the phone, there have been no new announcements and they won't say much about it when I ask, just "Nothing new" rather than the more traditional "No comment". The Inspector went back to his base in Chelmsford a while ago and my best contact at the local station now is with Sergeant Jane, I think she would help if she could but there's clearly no real leads.

What do I know? Evidently no one was found to have more than a vague memory of seeing a man dressed as Father Christmas at the prize giving in the library, speaking for myself I couldn't begin to describe what the man was like. Similarly nor did anyone recall seeing the children go out from the event. There are also evidently no clues about the car used to drive the children away, either at the library or at the rented house where the children were held; where is a nosey parker writing down number plates when you need one? The kids only remember the car as a dark coloured estate, which doesn't even begin to narrow it down; I happen to know the commonest car colour in the country is a highly imaginative grey. Besides given the quality of their family cars the kids probably just felt uncomfortable. To the best of my knowledge there were no fingerprints found either, well, apart from my own that is, and for sure none that help and link to someone with a criminal record, I am not sure which it is, but Sergeant Jane let that one slip. I imagine it is the same with regard to DNA: if any was found that might belong to the kidnapper, then there is nothing else to which to link it. If anything like this had produced a useful clue then I am sure we would have heard about it by now.

For all his denials, I remain pretty sure that Kent had paid a ransom when I spoke to him outside his house, but there has been nothing else to substantiate it as a fact, while it is only a hunch on my part anyway, he did look very uncomfortable at the time. Not quite the right word: the dictionary defines uncomfortable as "uneasy; causing or feeling disquiet" and I think uneasy fits the bill rather better. He definitely looked increasingly uneasy during that conversation. Still there have not to my knowledge been any further clues to show whether this idea could be right or wrong. Kent is clearly saying nothing and I'm sure as heck whoever the kidnapper is won't be issuing a statement any time soon. It's intriguing, but it gives me nothing new I can report on and, with no evidence at all, I have never mentioned my feeling to the police.

What else is there? The kids saw very little, they only remembered the man's disguise, he spoke to them only briefly and they noticed no pronounced accent or any other distinguishing feature. Even if he had a dramatic tattoo on his face or neck, the false beard covered everything. I imagine the house gave up no clues, though I presume the police must have found out how it was rented from the owner, but nothing useful seems to have come from that either. I know that the police have spent some time on the link with Kent's company and the various messages and threats sent to them about their new drug being too expensive. If that has led to knocks on any doors I have heard nothing of it identifying suspects, and the senders of the many emails and social media messages were located all around the world so I am sure most, if not all, of those can be firmly ruled out. However aggrieved, rude or threatening someone in, say, Singapore, was I don't suppose they turned up in Maldon Library dressed as Santa Claus. For all I know the police are still sifting through hundreds of such messages, a job made even harder by the fact that the most aggressive were doubtless mostly anonymous, something no doubt especially true of those on social media. Indeed social media must complicate much police work no end these days.

It's been quite a week for me. Good to look back on as I go about the daily grind: currently I have to write up a story about a kid raising money for the local air ambulance (worthwhile, I guess), another about the lack of people being fined for not picking up their dogs' mess on a footpath near a school (also worthwhile in a way, if it makes people change their ways – but of course cynical little me doubts it will) and I must contact the electricity company about a car accident that brought down a power line causing cuts over quite a wide area. Actually I do notice a change since Smaug (I think he'll stay Smaug for the moment) gave me full reign with the kidnap story. A little less checking on me, a little more autonomy and better stories to get my teeth into. I have just got one about a significant planning issue and been asked to see that right through over what might be many months of planning applications, appeals, protests and ultimately some conclusion. Better, definitely better.

In the immediate aftermath of my child rescue exploits the kidnap story made all the national press, I was able to shadow John and learn a good deal more about how to liaise with and sell a story to other news outlets. This not only made our paper some money, which put a contented smile on Smaug's face, at least for a while, it also adds to my knowledge in a useful way.

I don't think there is a single national that has not had my name in it, more than once for most; the same goes for Margaret. Photos too. Happily the kids are safe, they were featured too, of course, although Elizabeth was very protective of them; maybe they will begin to forget all about it now. I am glad I phoned Elizabeth and got reassuring news. For the moment the trail has apparently gone as cold as a penguin's toes in terms of finding out who did it and so, with no sign of any development that will change that, the story has pretty much faded away. Several of my pieces in the local paper were given prominent place and Smaug even insisted on my own role being featured more strongly than the way in which I had originally positioned it. All good for my scrapbook, though I have promised myself I will get my hair cut – a resolution prompted by seeing so many photos of myself.

My mother has a subscription to the *Express* and must, as predicted, have phoned me ten times in the days that followed the reporting of the incident both before and after my visit home. Her congratulations were regularly interspersed with horror and disapproval for my "having put yourself at such risk". It's a little odd doing a job which allows others to follow the detail of what you are up to in as much detail as mine does. Now I live further away both my parents take advantage of this and will often have a comment about stories I have been involved in. This was certainly a big story and since then a good many people have recognised me as I've walked through the town during the last few days. Maybe Margaret has had the same, I must ask her about it. I bet she has had comments in the Library where, of course, she regularly has face to face contact with the public.

Fame at last, though doubtless such fame will fade fast – as too does having these few quiet moments to pause for reflection.

*

"Alice, in here please." A shout. Smaug. Abrupt as ever... but, hey, wait a minute, he said *please*: what's that all about for goodness sake? I get up and weave my way through the open plan office to his lair. He watches me through the glass wall as I walk towards him.

"Come in, come in. Have a seat." I see that for once one chair is already free of files and sit down. I'm finding his sudden politeness to be rather unnerving, perhaps he's had a rudeness bypass, and I'm wondering whatever may be going to come next.

"You know what date it is today." That doesn't quite seem to be a fully formed question, but yes I do know, this near to Christmas most people will know that. The holiday means a smaller size for the paper this week so we all have a bit more time. When I say nothing in reply he continues.

"I must apologise." Oh, good grief, unusual politeness and now an *apology*, what on Earth is going on? Has the dragon's fire somehow got dampened down a bit?

"It's been a bit hectic around here lately, as you know much better than most, and I'm afraid I have let your job review date go by unremarked." Unremarked. Good word, a brief entry in the dictionary says "without mention, unnoticed". I ponder this as I realise that it had for sure been unremarked on by me. For the moment, given other things going on, it had slipped out of my mind completely. I must be looking blank.

"Had you forgotten about it too, you're on a six month trial period, remember?"

"Yes, of course, sorry. It has been pretty full on over the last few days." At any other time I would have remembered such a landmark, and I would have been wondering about it also, but the last little while has been, well, he said hectic and he's right, though I'm not sure why I am apologising for having had my mind on other things. I reckon my focus on the job is usually very good.

"No need to apologise, but we do need to do something about it. Now - do I take it you would like to stay on?" I do not hesitate.

"Yes, of course... I hope you will want me to."

"Indeed yes, I certainly do. I need to conduct a formal job appraisal meeting with you of course, all that employment legislation malarkey makes that mandatory, but we can have that meeting later, it will wait until after Christmas. First, let me say that you have been very patient, it takes a while to get run in to this sort of work, and you have not only spent six months doing all the dogsbody jobs without complaint, but I can see you have paid attention. You've learnt a lot and you do the job well. Very well." Well that's all right enough so far, I reckon. He pauses for a moment, but I just wait, saying nothing.

"Then there was this kidnap story. I know a little luck was involved, if Jake had not got given that smart watch, things might have been different." He's right about that, of course, and here was me thinking it was all my exceptional creative thinking, journalistic and investigative nous, anyway he did get the watch and I did find the instructions.

"That apart I have to say that you rose to the occasion with a vengeance, you've probably researched and written more about all this than you wrote in any of the previous six months... and it was all good."

Yes, right, now I think about it, none of my stuff has come back with red marks all over it for quite a while now. For some reason, it's a sign I never really consciously noticed before. I concentrate, I try to look humble and grateful, and I push my glasses up my nose. Damn it – again, I must curb this habit. There's clearly more to come. He only pauses for a second and I let him continue.

"Anyway I need to confirm your appointment on a permanent basis, as a fully-fledged reporter, in writing, it changes the terms and conditions of your contract, more holiday for instance - I'll give Becky the details and get her to prepare formal written confirmation. How does that sound?" It sounds very good. I may still regard working on a local paper as a first step, but this is definite progress and I can't see me wanting to go anywhere else for a good while. After all my job seems to growing all the time at present. So he's not all grump. Indeed I assume this did not come out of the blue, he has clearly been monitoring my progress carefully. If I remember right the fictional Smaug had a weakness that was his downfall, maybe Bob's weakness is a good story. After this I may even have to find a new name for him in future, though thinking of him as that is a habit I might find difficult to break. I give him my most grateful smile.

"Good, yes, thanks very much." I am tempted to gush a bit, but successfully resist doing so.

"Well, welcome aboard… properly." He smiles back and I get up to go back to my desk. As I get half way out of his office door and am turning to pull it to I see him beckoning me back.

"Oh, one more thing, your salary increases a bit too." He names a figure that is a genuine surprise to me and, while it is still not a fortune, it is a real improvement; my immediate thought is that it will make me much better able to afford the new flat share.

"Thank you, that's really…" He saves me from having to think of the right phase in response by raising a hand and interrupting me.

"I do have to insist on one condition though… just wipe that face off the sign on my office door will you!" He's really not so bad after all, I think our relationship is future is going to be a whole lot better.

"Yes, boss."

CHAPTER THIRTY TWO
Do not leave unattended

Mary McKeith was a life-long helper – a volunteer extraordinaire – the kind of person that every community needs. Asked to raise money, staff a stall at a church fete or bake a sponge cake for a W.I. sale, she was always amongst the first in line to sign up. Provided, as she told everyone, it was a cause of which she approved. At present her main regular job was working as a volunteer assistant for two morning shifts a week at the Farreach Hospice shop at the Bentalls Centre in Heybridge on the edge of Maldon. She lived in a small terraced house in Heybridge Basin and, when the weather permitted, it was sufficiently near for her to walk along the canal to the shop, something that gave her a bit of exercise and sometimes allowed her to have a bit of a chat with some of those fishing along the canal bank. Such people would usually exchange a cheery word, though she rarely saw anyone catch a fish. It was a route along which she regularly walked her dog, Betty, though on mornings when she was to be working at the shop her canine companion had to remain at home.

One of her jobs, one of the jobs that occurred regularly in any charity shop, was to take in, acknowledge and sort the donations of items that came into the shop. Most they were pleased to get, but a few were rejected, for instance she wondered what made some people think that a battered and burnt out old saucepan that they regarded as being overdue for replacement would be snapped up by someone else and command a useful price. Something she always had to remember was to ask if people were Gift Aided: that is if they were tax payers and thus their donation fitted in with a government scheme effectively making their donation worth more to the charity. This was something not everyone knew about and even if they did they might not realise what a significant difference it made, one very much worth an extra moment in the shop to record it. Of course thanks were in order too, not just a simple thank you, but a few words making clear just how much funds were needed and thus that donations were very much appreciated. Many people who came into the shop were regulars both in donating and buying. It was a chatty environment amongst both volunteers and shoppers and she enjoyed her shifts no end.

Only occasionally was it difficult. Some people, just a few, abused this sort of thing. Occasionally rambunctious children had to be chased out of the shop or a polite but firm word had with their parents before they could do any damage and, less often, someone would try to make off with something without paying. Really thought Mary, surely stealing, say a blouse priced at what was typically a very modest amount compared to a regular shop, from a charity was both a heartless and stupid act, or were some people really that desperate? Sometimes it made her wonder. One thing that was a perennial issue was that regularly some people left bags containing donated items on the doorstep before the shop was open for business in the morning. Everyone was told not to do that, there was a "do not leave unattended" notice on the door and those making donations were regularly reminded about it. Mary thought some people might have good reason for so doing: if they went to work then it might be impossible for them to drop off donations when the shop was open and thus this was their only way of making a contribution; in that case their not breaking the rule might risk a donation being missed. But the practice could make problems and there were sometimes unfortunate incidents of such bags being stolen before they could be brought safely into the shop. A pretty low trick that was she reckoned.

Today, though chilly, it was a bright morning and she had walked along the canal at a brisk pace, enjoying the winter sunshine, but wearing a thick coat to keep warm against the cold December day. She had met no one and thus she found herself a few minutes early arriving at the shop. She did not have a key so she waited patiently for Doris her colleague to arrive, noting as she did so that today was one of those days when a couple of bags had been left on the doorstep. Some people, she thought, but also reckoned, never mind – because, after all, every donation helped. And anyway these two bags were not going to get stolen now that she was there to keep an eye on them. The car park and other shops alongside were quiet, most of the other shops around had also yet to open, only a few cars were in the carpark and a single person was standing outside waiting for the Post Office to open, this made Mary think that it was probably too late to be posting anything you hoped to arrive before Christmas. The nearest car was occupied by a man who appeared to be on his phone. The low sun was reflecting off his windscreen and making it difficult to see, but he appeared to be speaking on a mobile phone and, as he held the phone to his ear, she got the distinct impression that he was watching her; but the car was a little way off and her eyesight was not all that it once was.

"Morning Mary, sorry to keep you waiting." A voice at her elbow interrupted her thoughts: her colleague had arrived and with her the key to the door.

"Hello Doris, don't apologise, you are right on time and I've only been here a moment or two, it's a lovely crisp morning and I walked along the canal."

Doris put the key in the lock, opened the door and each grabbing one of the doorstep donation bags, they both went inside, pleased to find the shop already warm. Mary hooked the strap of her handbag over her shoulder to free a hand and turned the sign on the door from Closed to Open as she went inside, noticing as she did so that the man in the car had put his phone away and was, she thought, still watching her. As she stared back the car reversed back and just as it began to drive away she thought the man smiled and gave her a thumbs up sign. Well, she was getting on a bit for being propositioned, she thought, but it was difficult to see as the car got further away, anyway, of course, it was likely not to have been directed at her. She went through to the back office, put the bag up onto the sorting table and took off her coat. She collected the other bag from where Doris had put it on the counter and put it alongside the other.

"Put the kettle on please, will you Mary," her colleague called out as she got the till working, "I'll only be a minute."

Mary set the kettle boiling, laid out a couple of rather battered mugs, donations that had not been good enough to put on sale, and got the milk she had brought from home out of her own bag, and then went to the bag she had brought in from outside the shop. It looked the same as the one her colleague had carried in, they were both strong plastic laundry bags with red, white and blue stripes on them. They very much appeared to be new and bags were always welcome, they never had enough, and any that came in could always be reused. These ones weighed a good deal and she had found it an effort to hoist hers up onto the table. She thought they probably contained books, such were amongst the heaviest things given to the shop, though not the most profitable and they tended to get multiple copies of the most popular titles and authors. Or maybe it was china or glass, which could also be heavy, though no chinking sound indicated that. Looking more closely she saw that each of the bags contained several packages inside, each one separately wrapped neatly in brown paper. A typed note stuck on top of each said simply: "Thank you for all you do. Hope this helps. No publicity about this please." The last few words were in capital letters, thus giving a clear message, though that did not seem to make much sense and she wondered why the phrase had been included.

There was no clue to the contents. When Mary went to the first bag and began to tear the paper away from the topmost packet her mouth dropped open, closing it again she then muttered under her breath: "Well, that's not something you see every day." Quite an understatement as she found herself looking at bundles of bank notes constituting more money than she had ever seen before in her whole life. She found it almost unbelievable, but there it was and a quick check suggested that the entire contents of the bag were the same. After taking it in for a moment she called through to the shop.

"Doris, come and have a look at this, you will simply *never* believe it."

*

Not long after the two ladies had discovered the money Gerald Davies was back home enjoying what he regarded as a well-earned cup of tea. He didn't feel this last stage of his plan had posed any risk, though he had waited outside the shop to make sure that nobody made off with the bags before the shop opened. He had watched them be safely taken inside before he drove off. He could not be seen to have a part in this, of course he couldn't, but he had so wished he could have seen the faces of the two ladies who had taken in the bags when they opened them up to check what had been donated. All in all he felt that his plan had been a success and he had been especially pleased to read in the local newspaper that the kids seemed to be none the worse for their experience. He now realised that he had been lucky though, things had not gone completely to plan and he would never have thought about the boy's watch in a month of Sundays. He was not sufficiently up on such things to even know that was a possibility and that lack of knowledge could have seen him be caught. The timing had been tight too, though timing had always been crucial. So far as he could make out, having discovered that the Kent kids had gone, he must have left the house perhaps only minutes before the police arrived on the scene.

All in all he felt he had not only been successful, his plan had worked, even if a measure of luck had been involved, but looking back he had also actually rather enjoyed it. His life was somewhat dull and predictable now he was retired and he wondered what else he could find to do to add a bit of excitement. As he did so he found himself calling to mind Michael Caine's famous last line in the film "The Italian Job" spoken as the coach and its on board gold hung precariously on the cliff edge: *Hang on a minute lads. I've got a great idea.*

He wondered what other ideas he might come up with.

It was still early, too early for a real drink, but he allowed himself a celebratory chocolate digestive biscuit with his tea – even though he would not regard the plan as all over quite yet. He still hoped for a final important piece of news.

EPILOGUE
The most surprising thing

It's been a long day, more to do and better things to do; Smaug has been as good as his word. I really am feeling like a proper reporter these days. Today it's been especially hectic during the last couple of hours, I haven't stopped for what seems like an age, I need a good stretch after sitting too long at my keyboard and frankly I could now murder a cup of tea. But I'm done now, at least for today, I put on my coat, say goodbye to Becky who is still busy at the reception desk and leave the office. I am headed for Salty Dogs. This is, I am told, something of an annual tradition in Maldon, a shop run and stocked by a group of local artists, only open over the Christmas period, it stocks everything from pictures to ceramics to books and cards. I need a present for my mother who will be providing me with my Christmas dinner come the day. Something from the town I now call home seems appropriate. However, that is not to be: as I step out onto the High Street pavement I am immediately accosted. No, the dictionary would tell me that's not the right word, particularly for this polite request. Perhaps greeted is a better word.

"Hello there, Alice, I wonder if you can spare me a minute?" I do a double take then recognition dawns, the lady in front of me is Mary McKeith of lost dog recovery fame, though the dog in question is mercifully not with her at the moment, it was a nasty yappy little thing as I recall. I am quite proud of myself for recognising her, the dog incident was a little while back and rather more important things have happened to me since then. I am due to meet Margaret at the flat for supper in due course, but at the moment, if I leave the present buying for another time, I have plenty of time.

"I guess I do, yes, how can I help?"

"I'd like to buy you a cup of tea, do you have time to walk down to Mrs Salisbury's? They do a very good cake there and, if you don't mind my saying so, you look as if you need feeding up my dear." Having concluded that I have nothing pressing on for the moment, a cup of tea is anyway high on my list and cake sounds good too, so I say yes and we set off together down the road. I am as susceptible to cake as the next person especially if I have just been told I am of a size that readily allows for some. She leads the way a few yards down the High Street and turns left along an alleyway: Bright's Path. Not only do I know this is named after Edward Bright, a citizen of Maldon in the mid-seventeen hundreds, who was known as "The fat man of Maldon" and reputed to be the fattest man in England, I am pleased to see that the sign has been painted with the correct apostrophe. Pedants like me were appalled not only by the decline in its correct usage, but also by the Apostrophe Protection Society recently closing down, defeated as its founder said at the time by "ignorance and laziness".

I follow Mary into the tea shop. Maybe she has something to say that will give me another story; perhaps she is becoming an informant, one of my "sources" as we reporters say, now there's an intriguing thought. She is clearly a regular here and is greeted as such. Now settled at a corner table, with tea and Victoria Sponge on order, I want to find out what she wants.

"I hope your dog's not gone missing again, Mary." This was our only point of contact so it seems to make a reasonable point at which to start.

"No, it's something completely different." She pauses and furrows her brow as if struggling for words then continues. "I wonder, can I speak to you 'off the record', I hope that's the right phrase. I think this is something that should remain confidential, strictly between you and me. Is that okay?" Well, I would never have thought of her as being an "off the record" kind of person, so I am now both intrigued and doubly keen to know what this is all about. Our conversation pauses for a moment while a waitress delivers our order, the cake certainly looks to be a wonderful treat.

"Yes, we can regard it that way if you want, I guess, and yes that certainly sounds like the right phrase." I resist saying how incongruous I find her saying it.

"That's good my dear, how's the cake." I sense this might take a little time, I cut off a bite sized bit of sponge and give it a try, nodding with enthusiasm as I eat it: my "Mmmm" comes with no contrivance.

"You did so well with that kidnap business, you know, I read all about it, just wonderful, and so good those poor children came to no harm. Are they really okay now?"

"Well, I actually telephoned Elizabeth Kent very recently for an update. They did have a scary time, of course, but yes, I'm pleased to say that it all finished up well for them in the end. No bad lasting effects and they were even able to keep the bikes." She nods, she clearly did read all about it and knows about the bikes. I take another bite of cake as she continues speaking.

"Has it all ended though? I mean are there any signs that the police will catch the perpetrator?"

"Not really, no. I am beginning to think they never will. It seems most likely what happened was an elaborate part of the protest about the supply of the cancer drug produced by James Kent's company being restricted because of its cost. The company has had hundreds of complaints from all over the world – some of them abusive – and threats too, so if it was done as part of that then it might be anyone and they might be anywhere."

"Yes, I read all about it, but I've not read anything about a ransom, surely they would have demanded money?"

"The police seem to think that the kids' getting away took place before a ransom could be demanded. But, well, don't quote me, but I think James Kent may have paid something and is saying nothing about it. It was not so much what he said to me as how he reacted to my suggestion of it, he didn't like that at all and looked very uncomfortable. But I've absolutely no proof he did, and of course as the kids escaped we can't know if something being paid would have seen them being released later on." I suddenly wonder - why am I telling her all this? She mustn't mention it - I wouldn't put it past Kent to sue me if my comment led to accusations.

"As I say, please don't say that to anyone, now it's me wanting to be off the record, it was probably just a silly idea, and the last thing I want is Kent hearing I said it."

"Quite so, my dear, quite so, but do you know what? The most surprising thing happened to me a few days ago." Clearly I don't know what and I say so. She continues. "Well, I'm a volunteer helper at a charity shop, just a couple of mornings a week, you know, but I like to think it all helps. I got there the other day before Doris, she has the key you know, and I had to wait a minute or two before going in. Anyway there were two bags already sitting on the doorstep. People doing that, leaving stuff plonked outside before we open, is a regular occurrence. We tell them not to, of course we do, and there are notices too because anyone could walk off with them, and that does happen sometimes. People stealing from a charity, awful isn't it? Anyway that morning there were two bags and what do you think was in them?"

"Aren't most donations clothes?"

"Yes indeed, mostly women's things, but not in this case, obviously not because these particular bags were much too heavy. It was... now, I have to be sure: this *is* off the record isn't it?" That phrase again, it still seems odd coming from my dog lady. She leans forward conspiratorially as she speaks, eager that no one else sitting nearby can hear her.

"I'm still not sure why, but yes I did say yes. So I promise it is 'off the record' as you put it."

"Well I was just flabbergasted. When I opened up one of the bags it was full of bank notes – cash – they both were." She pauses for effect and, surprised and stunned, I just wait for her to continue. "It proved to be an exact sum: £100,000 no less, in used bank notes and there was a little note stressing that there should be no publicity about it. That's something usually unheard of. Now, perhaps because I had met you and knew about your involvement with those children, this made me think. I thought it was quite a coincidence that this money was delivered just a few short days after the kidnapping took place. What do you think? I thought you would like to know about it, after all you did, you know, but I don't want anything to happen that might mean the money has to go back, you do understand that don't you? That's why it must remain between us." I'm astonished, which the dictionary says is amazed or greatly surprised, I think flabbergasted is a better word as that implies *overwhelming* surprise. Yes, flabbergasted with bells on. My face must be a picture. Though there is still no proof, but I bet this means I was right about James Kent paying a ransom - what a story this could lead to. But damn it it's one I have just promised not to tell, not ever, to anyone, and besides, if it was ransom money from the kidnapping and that's what *was* behind the whole thing, then I'm not sure I want anyone else to know either. Despite the circumstances I reckon I would regard it as a tragedy if the money had to be returned. If it's true then whoever was involved was a very curious kind of kidnapper indeed. I nearly swear, which I am sure Mary would not appreciate.

"Well… that's… well, it's *amazing*, what's more I think you could well be correct. It all ties together, not least with the care taken to minimise harm to the children. What charity does the shop belong to?" Mary explains. I may only have lived in this part of the world a short while, but I well know how highly the hospice is regarded locally. How should I view all this? Those poor kids had a scary time, but that was one hell of a donation for a charity to get. Think what they can do with that. The publicity from the crime may have been influencing the question of the drug pricing too.

"Well, I guess we'll probably never know if it was ransom money or not, Mary, I can't imagine any way it could be proved and neither James Kent nor the kidnapper are likely to say anything. But you know what? If you *are* right the kidnapper was, in part at least trying to do a good thing; it makes the whole episode very curious. I still feel for the kids, but I think I am entirely happy to regard this as our little secret,

I have to agree with you that the money should remain where it is. Thanks for confiding in me about it."

"Yes, indeed, I'm so glad we had this little chat. It does all seem to tie up doesn't it? Somehow I just had to tell someone, and I am pleased you agree. Now, will you let me get you some more cake, my dear?"

*

A week or so later the kidnap story has faded from both the national and local news. The children after all are safe, as far as I can gather the police have reduced their attention on the matter still more and nothing to do with it appears in the news or on my to do list any more, though I'm pleased to say that I have other stories to work on now. Last time that I inquired, Sergeant Jane told me simply that's she'd "heard not a whisper".

Whatever sort of investigation may be continuing at present, finding the kidnapper seems to me like a lost cause. Since my meeting with Mary McKeith I have my own theories about it all and this morning those were reinforced when I noticed that the national newspapers were all carrying the story that Demonaxx has made a sudden and unexpected agreement to re-price their controversial cancer drug and that it is now soon to be available on the NHS. The protest group Cure vs Cost are unsurprisingly claiming victory, saying that this "climb down" as they put it was the direct result of their campaign. Of course they are.

Certainly it's a positive result: one a great many people may benefit from - me, I think the change of heart is down to one curious individual who took some radically different action. Right now, reading the reports, he must be feeling pretty damn pleased with himself.

I'd like to think he wasn't all bad and I would so very much love to know who that person is.

END

AUTHOR'S NOTE (AND THANKS)

I have lived in the town of Maldon for more than twenty years. It is a place I love. The town has a Library, a Police Station and a local paper. All are good, but none are quite as depicted here: the people, circumstances and manner of working I describe are all fictitious and the real local paper is called *The Maldon Standard*.

Both my previous novels, *Long Overdue* and *Loose Ends,* are also set in the town and, while the basic geography and nature of the town are reflected with a degree of accuracy in all three, the details are fictitious. The same applies to the pharmaceutical company and cancer drug that play a part in this story. Farreach Hospice is not intended to be Farleigh Hospice, or reflect their operating procedures, though they do have two shops in Maldon one of which is at the Bentalls Centre. I have personal experience of the work of Farleigh, which is an organisation of which I simply cannot speak too highly – so any excuse to give them a mention – and perhaps encourage donations – I regard as not to be missed. Incidentally you can read one of my short stories in an anthology published to raise money for them: *A Great Little Gallimaufry* remains available as I write.

Writing is essentially a solitary activity. Certainly what writers call the BOSHOK stage – Bum on Seat, Hands on Keyboard is just that. But writing, like so much else, is fuelled by contact with others. I enjoy the company of other writers and belong to various writing groups including the Brentwood Writers' Circle, a body of some fifty members of which, as I write, I am Chairman. I am also one of the few male associate members of the SWWJ (Society of Woman Writers and Journalists) and a member of the Society of Authors. People from all of these and small writing groups too have all helped my writing both motivationally and technically.

I read a book recently that listed more than a hundred people in its Acknowledgements and I do not propose to copy that here. However many people helped directly or indirectly with this book, and under the directly heading I must mention particularly Jacqueline Connelly, always my first reader, and Lloyd Bonson publisher extraordinaire. For whatever the part others may have played, many thanks.

About The Author

Patrick Forsyth is the much published author of many non-fiction books. Many offer guidance to those working in organisations, for example *Successful Time Management* (Kogan Page) is a bestselling title on its subject. He has also written three light-hearted books of travel writing: *First class at last!, Beguiling Burma* and *Smile because it happened.* All are set in South East Asia.

Another title is the book *Empty when half full* a hilarious critique of miscommunication that misleads and amuses. He has had two novels published previously: *Long Overdue,* a light mystery concerning a missing person, and *Loose Ends,* a sequel. He is active in the writing world, writing regularly for *Writing Magazine* and working with several writing groups. He lives in Maldon in north Essex and this is his third novel.

Also from the Author

First Class At Last!
An Antidote to Past Travel Horrors
More Than 1,200 Miles in Extreme Luxury

Fed up with the strenuous process of travel: the slow queues, the delays, the crowds and the extreme discomfort of the average economy airline seat?

Patrick Forsyth decided it was time to do something about this. He arranged a trip designed to be the antidote to the routine travel misery - and booked a trip travelling only first class.

The first challenge was to decide where to go. He decided to fly to Bangkok, stay in the world renowned Oriental Hotel, continue onto Singapore and stay at the equally famous Raffles Hotel. He then travelled in style back to Bangkok on the Eastern and Orient Express, where he spent two nights on what many people regard as the best train ride in the world, and finally concluded his travel at a luxury spa on the beach, to recover.

Along the way, the author meets a rock and roll musician; visits dubious bars and colourful markets; has an encounter with the bodyguards of the Thai Royal Family; and embarks on a boat trip along the River Kwai. This lively, amusing account of luxury travel, highlights what every traveller secretly longs to do - travel in style and grandeur.

"...witty and full of facts ..." Essex Life

"... Lively, witty and wry." Select Books

"... it reminded me of Bryson..."
Neal Asher, bestselling author of Gridlinked

Long Overdue

By his own admission, Philip is living a humdrum life in the Essex coastal town of Maldon.

His new boss at the town library is a pain in the neck, making even the job he loves difficult, and he longs for something to kick start him out of what he admits is a bit of a rut. Soon after a new and unexpected friendship begins he determines to make some changes.

Then one day his routine walk to work has him finding a dead body, involved with the police and feeling he must help his new friend by investigating a mystery from years past.

As events following the death carry him along, an abandoned sailing boat, half a letter and a surprising alliance sees him seeking to unravel the mystery of a missing person.

He quickly realises that dialling the emergency services that spring morning is leading to changes that will affect his life, his job and his future as well as having him travel abroad and make some surprisingly impulsive decisions

"Patrick Forsyth has written many non-fiction books but this is his first novel. It comes with a real ear for dialogue and a pulse-quickening sense of risk. As for Philip, he is a thoroughly well-rounded protagonist for whom you root from the start."
The Good Book Guide

Novels:

Long Overdue

Loose Ends

Humour:

Empty when half full: *a compendium of, and comment on, bizarre communications*

Travel writing:

First class at last!

Beguiling Burma

Smile because it happened

All three light-hearted travel books are set in South East Asia, the first involving a train journey, the second a river trip and the third is about various aspects of Thailand (the so-called land of smiles) all likely to make you smile.

Other Fiction from Stanhope Books

A Higher Authority – *Barrie Hyde*

A young Oxford graduate with a gift for languages joins MI5 and is then seconded to 'A Higher Authority', an organisation funded through government sources from around the world which nobody would admit to.

Countries have to be seen to be playing it straight, and sometimes can't get at the bad guys. This is where 'The Organisation' comes in.

Our hero is given the code name Jonathan to 'avoid contagion' and trained at an old British Army camp in Kenya, where he meets and falls in love with his Zan, a Chinese colleague.

Catapulted into the world of industrial espionage their mission is to find out from the inside how a company has been able to grow at lightning speed. They find themselves embroiled in kidnapping, murder, drug running and money laundering.

Watermelon Man – *Peter Norman*

Regaining consciousness late at night in a dark alleyway in a strange town, the man realises that he has been mugged and robbed of everything—including his memory!

He begins a journey that turns from a dream into a nightmare as nothing is as he had hoped it would be.

Forced to confront his demons, his problems collapse into a web from which there appears to be no escape . . .

BV - #0018 - 301020 - C0 - 203/127/12 - PB - 9781909893290 - Gloss Lamination